Isla

Annie Seaton

Pentecost Island 10

ANNIE SEATON

Prologue
Pippa

'We're ready to go, girls,' I said as I opened the gate to the new pool area on Pentecost Island. Tamsin and Nell, my two best friends in the whole world—after my husband, of course—followed me onto the new lawn. Our island was being tagged on social media as the island of love, so Valentine's Day morning was an appropriate day to open our new infinity pool.

'Oh, my freakin' God, the pool has water in it,' Tam squealed.

'Of course it does,' I said with a smile. 'Did you think Zac was going to jump into an empty pool?'

Rafe and I had decided to have the pool filled late yesterday afternoon so that it was a surprise for the staff when they walked across to the infinity pool by the water's edge behind the huts this morning.

'Look at those incredible day beds.' Nell clapped her hands in almost childish delight. 'I want to have a holiday here.'

'You live here, Nelly,' Tam said with a grin.

'I know, but what a place to have a holiday!'

I reached out and linked my arms through my friends' arms. 'We've done good, gals. We've *all* done good.' I sent a quick thank-you up to my Aunty Vi who'd left me the island last year, and now we'd planned and almost completed what was becoming a high-demand resort. Bookings were at full capacity, and we were booked ahead for months, even though it was the low tourist season in North Queensland. My only worry was the weather, but our new facilities had been built to cyclone standard. The original house—my great-aunt Vi's dwelling—had survived cyclones, Ada and Debbie, in the past, so I was confident we could ride the next one out when it came, as we knew it would.

A crowd had gathered around the new pool. I was pretty sure every guest in the resort had turned up for the opening. The water glinted in the morning sunlight; the weather gods had put on a spectacular day for us. The expanse of the Whitsunday Passage towards the mainland was the usual sapphire blue, dotted with white sails as bareboat yachts enjoyed the paradise that the Whitsunday Islands offered. Being a part of a business that provided a holiday destination to those who needed a recharge was very satisfying. Just looking at that body of water created calm in the most troubled soul.

I knew that very well.

Sitting on the balcony in our house up on the hill, looking out over the Passage over the past few weeks had contributed to my healing. I had healed fast physically, but the emotional toll from losing our baby was hard to deal with.

The morning was hot and humid and many of the guests were already in their swimming costumes, keen to have a dip as soon as the pool was officially open. Especially those who would be departing on the late morning launch. Our official "first splash" was at nine a.m. before the sun was too hot, although we had provided lots of shade around the perimeter of the pool, and—as Nell described them—incredible daybeds. Large enough for a small family, if needs be, and with soft mattresses and cerise-pink privacy curtains. Also, holding the "splash" early meant all the staff could be there to be a part of the celebration before they started work for the day.

Angus, our head chef had started breakfast half an hour earlier this morning, and Cherry, his partner, and assistant chef, had created fruit trays to go with the champagne cocktails. I could see the colourful array of tropical fruit lined up along the bar counter.

All our staff, present and former, were on the island this week. Evie and Jed had come across from their property south of Airlie Beach where Jed's rustic furniture business was doing very well. Evie, who had been our first landscaper, had helped Dylan—her replacement—with the final work over the past week. Like everyone else who'd been touched by Pentecost Island, she found it hard to stay away.

It was good to see Evie looking so happy since she and Jed had sorted out their marital misunderstanding. She and Dylan had done a superb job with the landscaping around the pool. Where there had once been a flat sandy area edged with dark rocks on the shore prior to the pool going in, full grown tropical shrubs in bloom now created a lush backdrop edging the paths and surrounding the new pool bar. Jed had completed a rush job of furniture for us and the new timber outdoor tables and chairs had arrived late last week.

Guests were beginning to leave comments in the guest book saying how beautiful the gardens on our island were and how the landscaping had added to their overall five-star experience. I made a mental note to thank Dylan and Evie for their work.

I smiled again and my gaze swept over the assembled group waiting as Rafe and Zac walked to the edge of the infinity pool. Rafe was doing the official bit this morning; I'd been so emotional since I'd lost our baby, I still didn't trust myself to speak in public and keep it together. Zac, our new lifeguard was doing the honours for the "official opening".

I chuckled quietly as I thought back to the girls' sunset drinks on the beach last week. Friday night drinks and a debrief at the end of each week had become an institution that Tam, Nell and I had started at the end of our first week on the island.

'I have a task for you, ladies,' I'd said as I stood on the high rock and looked down at my group of friends. 'We need someone to do the official jump into the pool and the first lap next week. Do we need to vote who it should be?'

Odessa's plummy voice rose over the soft swishing of the waves on the sand. 'Really, Phillipa darling, that is a no-brainer.'

A few months ago, I would have bristled at her tone, but I knew Odessa well enough now not to take any offence. 'A no-brainer? Does that mean you vote for your Dylan?'

She waved a languid hand, and I noticed that she was wearing some of the new pieces of jewellery she'd made to stock in our new boutique. 'As much as I think Dylan is the best-looking man on the island, it has to be Zac, as the lifeguard.'

Tess, Nell's relatively new assistant in the office, blushed as everyone agreed and the winning vote was cast for Zac.

Zac had brought Tess back over to the island two weeks ago, the day before I flew to Brisbane with Nell and Tamsin to select our dresses for Nell's wedding. Rafe and I had been on our balcony when he drew my attention to the couple who had come in by tender to our wharf.

I looked down as Zac took Tess into his arms and kissed her thoroughly, and then my gaze lifted to the white cruiser moored outside the bay.

A soft sigh had escaped my lips. 'Another happy couple on our island.'

'The "island of love" hashtag that guest created is pretty accurate,' Rafe said.

Zac and Tess had been inseparable ever since, and Zac's boat was now a permanent feature moored outside our bay. To our surprise once he'd sorted the past misunderstandings with Tess, Zac had asked if he could stay on and continue with the lifeguard and bar job.

'We both want to stay here, Pip,' Tess said. 'That is, if you're happy to have us. We love Pentecost Island.'

'Of course, we are,' I assured them. 'We don't want you to go anywhere. But Zac are you really sure you want to *work* here?'

Zac taking the job had originally been to track Tess down and convince her that he loved her. He had been successful, and they were now a happy couple, but considering he was a very wealthy man, I was surprised that he wanted to be our pool lifeguard and that they were going to stay.

'I want to be a part of your venture, Pippa. It's such a special place. We'll cruise around the islands on our days off,' Zac said. 'Eliza and Phillipe have told us about some of the great spots to moor. We've got seventy-four islands to explore.' He looked at me intently. 'And if you ever want to expand and need a silent partner, I'd like to put my hand up.'

Eliza, who had also bought into the island, and her partner, Phillipe, were spending less time cruising the islands these days, and I suspected that they were going to build a house on our island.

I glanced across to my two best friends beside me. Nell and Tamsin had been busy looking at house plans with our builders, the Riccardos, as well as both preparing for their babies who were due in the middle of the year. I pushed away that little bit of sadness that was always in my heart, and my sigh didn't get past eagle-eyed Tamsin.

'Why the sigh, Pip?' Tamsin's gaze was intent. No one apart from Rafe knew about the miscarriage.

'A happy sigh,' I forced a smile. 'Another love story on our island. Look at the way Tess is looking at Zac.'

Tam's voice was dry. 'Any living, breathing woman would look at Zac Montgomery like that. He's extremely easy on the eye.'

'Zac looks a bit self-conscious,' Nell said.

'And Tess looks smitten,' I added.

Tess and Cherry faced each other across the pool each holding an end of the bright pink ribbon. Rafe was going to cut the ribbon, and then Zac—looking very tanned and muscular—was to dive into the pool and swim the short lap. Phillipe was taking the photos for us to mark the occasion.

My brief melancholy lifted, and happiness filled me again as I looked around at the staff.

My friends. Each and every one of them.

Gabe and Nat came across to stand beside Tam and Nell. Eliza, Evie and Jed, Odessa and Dylan, Sienna and Danny stood together across from us. Angus was behind the bar ready to pop the champagne corks when Zac hit the water. Renzo Riccardo, our builder and his wife, were chatting to Angus; they'd come across from their home on Hamilton Island, so they'd be here for the opening too. As I thought about it, I realised that the love that everyone had for our island was the key to it being a huge success. And we would celebrate that again today.

One thing we did well on Pentecost Island was put on a celebration.

I was very pleased with the camaraderie between the staff. Even Odessa had settled in, and to my surprise, was becoming a close and loyal friend. Her wicked sense of humour had lifted my spirits a few times lately.

Our island was almost complete.

I was almost complete.

I had recovered physically and emotionally from my miscarriage and was looking forward to being pregnant again soon. I had faith that it would happen, and I had managed to shed my doubts with Rafe's love and support. I believed that a baby, the first in our future family would be the next step to strengthening our life on this island.

As far as the development of the business side of things went, the island was buzzing. Plans were well underway, and we were all looking forward to Nell and Nat's wedding in two weeks, not to mention the two babies on the way.

We would have a full complement of staff by then. I'd interviewed Isla O'Sullivan by phone, and Sienna's glowing praise of her work skills had been enough for me to offer her a twelve-month contract. I was still wary of the unknown though, and there was a month-long probation period. Sienna was excited about the arrival of her friend who was due to arrive on Jiminy's launch this morning.

'Excited, Pip?' Tamsin leaned in and interrupted my thoughts. 'Or daydreaming again?'

'Excited. And content.' I said, meeting her gaze steadily. I glanced down at her pregnant bump that seemed to be growing bigger every day.

'Good.'

'What about you?'

'Tired, but I'm good too.'

Nell nudged us to be quiet. 'Ssh, you pair, Rafe's about to start the official stuff.'

Rafe held the microphone up and a delicious shiver ran down my spine as my husband's deep voice, with his sexy posh accent, interrupted the happy conversations around us.

'Are we ready?' Rafe spoke over the portable PA system we'd brought in from the restaurant bar. He and Zac stood in the middle of the narrow walkway between the pool and the bar.

I flashed a thank-you smile at him; being an author—a famous author, I must add—he was excellent with the written word, but Rafe hated speaking in public. I knew his speech would be short and sweet.

'Good morning all, on this beautiful Whitsunday morning. Welcome to our guests, and our staff.'

The crowd quietened.

'I know you're all keen to try out our incredible new infinity pool, not to mention those inviting day beds, so it gives me great pleasure to declare Ma Carmichael's pool open. Zac, over to you.'

Yep, he was short and sweet, and I loved him for it.

I glanced over at Tess as Zac stepped up onto the short springboard. The love on her face kept the smile on my lips.

Zac walked to the end of the board and stood on his toes. He looked up and lifted a hand to his mouth and blew a kiss to Tess. I nodded as a sigh came from most of the women in the crowd. He sure *was* a fine-looking man. Zac's bronze tan was accentuated by his white boardshorts, but despite the collective admiration, his eyes sought only Tess's as he stood, poised on his toes on the edge of the walkway.

As Zac executed a perfect dive into the pool, a cheer went up and the popping of champagne corks came from the bar. We'd all agreed it wasn't too early to celebrate the pool opening with mimosas, and each guest was being given a complimentary drink in honour of the occasion. Dylan, Nat and Angus were soon walking around with trays of orange juice and champagne, and Cherry placed a tray of tropical fruit on each of the tables.

A horn sounded and I looked across to the east of the bay. Jiminy's launch was in earlier than usual.

I stared at the tall girl with dark curly hair who stood on the top of Jiminy's wheelhouse and waved madly, yelling out at the top of her voice. 'Helloooo, I'm here.'

'Sienna,' I called over the noise of conversations, 'Isla's arrived.'

Chapter One

Isla moved from the front of the boat where she'd kept a running commentary going since Pentecost Island had come into view.

'Oh, my sweet Lord, what a glorious island.' Taking a deep breath, she tried to fill her energy well so she could keep going when she greeted Sienna, and when she finally met the famous Pippa of Pentecost Island. Last night on Hamilton Island her sleep had been fractured by those old dreams, and each time she woke, self-doubt had gripped hold of her.

When they had been on Esculanta island, Sienna had commented on her confidence and wisdom. Isla rolled her eyes; she could have set Sienna straight, but no one would ever know the truth; she was far from wise. If she had half the wisdom and experience she pretended to have, her life choices would have been very different and her life would have been a lot easier. The *Isla* presented to the world was very different to the Isla within. It had been more than nine years since her world had shattered and she was beginning to think she would never get over it.

So, Isla had to keep the flamboyance going; and she would be Sienna's wise and exuberant friend from Esculanta Island and Pippa would think she was truly as wonderful as the performance she'd put on during the phone interview.

One day, who knew, maybe one day she could be herself again?

Oh, there was no doubt she could do this job. That was the one area of her life where Isla excelled. She was a very good therapist, and she enjoyed her work. The course on Esculanta Island had honed her deep tissue massage skills and she flexed her fingers as she thought of some of the new techniques she'd learned.

After they passed a luxurious white motor cruiser moored in the bay, they approached the wharf ahead where a huge black boat was secured to the end of the jetty, and Isla took another breath.

'Jesus, Mary, and Joseph! Will you look at that luxurious boat!' She put one hand to her chest and fanned her face with the other, broadening her Irish accent. She lifted her face to the sun and closed her eyes. 'Have I died and gone to heaven? A tropical island, palm trees and the boats of my dreams.'

When she was met with silence, Isla cracked one eye open, pleased to see that the rest of the passengers on the launch were focused on the island looming ahead of them, and the skipper—Jiminy, not a bad looking buff Aussie bloke wearing a wedding ring—was ignoring her, and concentrating on the narrow approach to the bay.

Being loud and getting in people's faces was a sure way to get ignored. Isla had tried the quiet and mysterious persona, but that just made observers more curious about you. Be an obnoxious loudmouth and people tended to steer clear and that suited her just fine. They didn't ask questions she didn't want to answer.

With a determined breath, she climbed onto the seat at the front of the boat, and put her arms out, pretending Leonardo di Caprio was behind her as they approached the wharf.

'I'm flying,' she called out.

No one replied, continuing to ignore her as they paid more attention to the island ahead. As the launch approached the jetty, Isla managed to distinguish Sienna's bright auburn hair among the crowd gathered together by a divine swimming pool.

'Helloooo, I'm here.' she called out, satisfied when heads turned.

***

Ronan Doyle stood beside the skipper of the launch and looked down at his watch. As soon as they'd disembarked, and he'd checked into his room, he was going to keep a low profile. He didn't want to come under the radar of the woman he'd been watching.

It would be better to disappear quietly and keep to himself until he had had a chance to check out the island, do some more research and figure out the best approach.

He still couldn't believe his luck. He'd searched for her for a long time, and in the end, the answer had fallen into his lap. Three countries, eight months and much investigation, and what had ensued was obviously meant to be. Serendipity, coincidence or just pure luck.

A chance meeting in Mission Beach, an overheard conversation, and he'd looked into the face of the woman he'd been hired to locate.

Call it what you like, but Ronan was sure in that moment he'd found the woman he'd been searching for over the past year.

The hardest thing was not reacting. He'd turned away in that Blues Bar in Mission Beach and pretended to be focused on the music. His connection had delivered, but he hadn't expected it to be so easy once he'd left Alaska. After he'd traced her there, she'd left and dropped off the radar for a few months. She'd changed her name—slightly—but this woman was a dead spit for the woman in the photo he carried in his wallet. The photo her sister had given him.

His biggest dilemma was not letting Isla O'Sullivan guess he was interested in her, because, as he well knew, she was a mistress of disappearing. He'd gone so close to tracking her down again in Cairns, and then the trail had run cold when he'd followed her to the resort on Esculanta Island. One day she'd been there, the next she was gone, and as far as he knew she hadn't caught either the plane or the launch to the mainland that day.

He would put his head down, and not open his mouth in front of her, because as soon as Isla heard his Irish accent she would be on her guard. The last thing he needed was for her to do a runner again.

He looked away as she squealed and waved to a red-headed woman waiting on the wharf.

Chapter Two
Dublin. Ten years earlier.

Aisling O'Sullivan jumped off the school bus without a backward glance. In the space of fifteen minutes since she'd boarded the bus in Castleknock, one of the posh suburbs of Dublin, she'd managed to change her clothes, trace her eyes with black kohl, load her lashes with mascara, and paint her lips with black lipstick.

The other girls had to dye their hair black, but Aisling was lucky. Her shoulder-length hair was naturally jet black, and her eyes didn't really need the kohl to tip them up at the corners. Having a Sri Lankan great-grandmother had given her a genetic advantage, but she still needed the clothes and the lipstick to fit in with her new group of friends.

'Well, look what we have here,' Brigid McGuire said as she pushed herself off the low whitewashed fence at the bus stop. The tall girl stubbed her cigarette against the wall before dropping the stub to the footpath.

'Aisling, you came.' Celia, Aisling's friend, grabbed her arm. 'You look gorgeous.' She lowered her voice to a whisper. 'A word of advice. Maybe don't look so good next time. Brigid won't like it.'

Aisling lifted her head and stared over tiny Celia's head to Brigid. 'Brigid will just have to get used to it, won't you, sweetie? You invited me to be a part of your group. You take me how I am. Or you don't take me at all. What do you have to say to that, girlfriend?'

Brigid shrugged and gestured to the other girl beside her. 'Something smells around here since the bus arrived. Come on, Dory, let's leave them to their boring selves.'

To her credit, Celia stayed with Aisling after the other two girls also dressed in black from head to toe disappeared around the corner.

'Oh, God, Aisling, what are we going to do now? They were going to take us to that club. Should we go back to school?'

'Looking like this? Can you image what Sister Mary would do? She'd have our parents in there in a flash. Besides, my sister already rang up and pretended to be my mam and said I was home with period cramps.' Aisling stared at Celia and reached into her pocket and pulled out a cigarette. 'You can go back to school, if you want to. I'm going to look for some fun. You can come or you can go. Your choice.'

Celia pulled herself up straight; she barely reached Aisling's shoulder. 'I'm coming. So where are we going?'

Aisling grinned at the tiny girl who had been her friend since the first day of prep school. '*Sanity* have a sale on and Da happened to leave fifty quid lying around this morning. Let's go buy some music.' The bitterly cold wind whistled down Tower Road and she pulled her black hoodie around her shoulders as she blew out cigarette smoke. 'And then we might go and look for some new Doc Martens.'

'I haven't got any money,' Celia said with a frown.

'There's ways to get around that,' Aisling said. She strode ahead as the wind blew rubbish around the street. Her parents and her sister, Marlene, deserved everything they got. She'd teach them to treat her as a second-class citizen.

Grounded, because she'd failed her stupid mathematics exam. Hauled over the coals and told she wasn't half the good girl that boring Marlene was. Although to be fair, Marlene had covered for her today. Aisling didn't care what trouble she got into. What were they going to do about it? She was their daughter. They'd chosen to have her, and if they didn't like what they got, they could live with it.

Same as the bitches who'd just left.

She was going to have fun, and she was going to do whatever she wanted.

Chapter Three
Pippa

I stood on the path at the side of the beach where Sienna had asked me to meet Isla when she got off the boat. As I watched them chatting, Jiminy spotted me and walked across the sand.

'Hey, Pippa. How's it going?'

I leaned over and kissed his cheek. Jiminy, the launch captain, had been my friend since high school when I lived up here on the island with Aunty Vi. 'Really good. You missed the pool opening. I was just standing over there thinking how well everything's going.'

'That's great. You've got some interesting guests just arrived on the launch.'

'Interesting?'

'Yeah, I guess you're bound to get some strange ones every now and then.'

'Interesting and strange? You have me intrigued.' I watched as two middle-aged couples and a guy by himself headed towards reception in the old house to check in. Tess had hotfooted it over there as soon as Zac had climbed out of the pool. 'Which ones? I'll let the staff know.'

He inclined his head towards the edge of the forest where the arriving guests had stepped onto the path. 'That guy's by himself. Couldn't get a peep out of him, not even a hello or an answer, just a nod when I held out my hand and introduced myself. He's bloody strange. Spent most of the trip perving on the other strange one. I even wondered if they were together and had had a fight.'

I shook my head. It was the most words I'd ever heard Jiminy say in one conversation, so I knew I'd better take heed. 'Which is the other strange one you're talking about?'

'The one who thought she was on the Titanic and never shut up the whole way. The two couples moved away and ended up ignoring her. That's her over there, she's waylaid Sienna.'

I groaned. 'Not that girl with the dark curly hair?'

'Yeah, that one.'

'That, my friend, is our new beauty therapist.' I rolled my eyes and stepped back towards the path. 'Thanks for the heads-up. I'll take close notice.'

'Good luck.' Jiminy grinned and headed over to the office to collect the guests who were departing this morning. I plastered a welcoming smile on my face and headed over to meet our newest staff member. If Jiminy was right and she didn't fit into our team she'd be gone after the month, even if Sienna didn't like it. I was surprised to hear what he'd had to say because Sienna had spoken so highly of Isla.

I would make my own judgment.

'Welcome to Pentecost Island, Isla.' I greeted her as she followed Sienna down the steps from the wharf. I held out my hand and held Isla's gaze steadily. 'I'm Pippa Rendell.'

A pair of intent dark eyes held mine just as steadily, and my first impression was of self-confidence. A warm and soft hand took mine in a firm grip and she smiled.

'Hello Pippa, it's lovely to meet you in person. I was just telling Sienna that the beauty of the island has rendered me speechless.' Her words seemed sincere, and her laugh was warm and attractive. If Jiminy hadn't warned me I would have been sucked right in then and there. Tam always told me I was a poor judge of character.

'I am just beside myself that I am going to be working here,' she said with a broad smile.

'We're very pleased to have you here.' I could lay it on thick too. Dropping her hand, I stepped back as Isla reached down to pick up a small suitcase.

'Do you have any other luggage, Isla?' Sienna asked.

'Just my big suitcase, and a couple of boxes of a new product I thought you might like to try in the spa, but Jim said not to worry because he would get them unloaded for me.'

As she answered Sienna, I checked Isla O'Sullivan out. She was certainly a stunning-looking woman. Her dark eyes were tipped up at the corners, but I suspected that look was enhanced by eyeliner, but it was hard to tell. Jet-black curls tumbled over her shoulders in wild abandon. Fair skin and rosy cheeks gave her a Snow White appearance; she was very beautiful.

'You'll be sharing my room in the old house just for a few days. I hope that's okay,' Sienna said as we crossed the beach to the path leading to the house. 'The new staff accommodation lodge up the hill is almost ready. Danny said he'd take us up to look at the rooms later today.' Sienna turned to me. 'If that's okay, Pippa?'

'Of course. I was up there yesterday, and the Riccardos have done a fine job. They're good enough to be used as resort rooms.'

Isla stopped and put one hand to her chest as we stepped out of the glade. 'Oh my lordy, what a sweet house. It reminds me of our little house in Dingle.'

'Dingle?' I asked.

'Yes, where I grew up in Ireland. The house wasn't as big as that one, and there were nine of us living there back in those days. I tell you what, it was a pleasure some days to go to school for peace and quiet. Oh Pippa, I haven't told you yet, but if I blather on too much, do tell me to put a sock in it. I'm used to trying to talk over my family, and sometimes I can run off at the mouth. I won't be offended.'

'I'll note that,' I said drily. I wondered how Odessa would take to our new arrival. Isla was certainly going to be an interesting addition to our team. Despite Jiminy's warning, I didn't see a problem . . . yet.

Chapter Four
Ronan

'Dinner is served in the restaurant from six p.m. but it's wise to let the staff know what time you'd like to eat.' The receptionist—Tess, according to her name tag—handed over a small pack of brochures along with his key. 'Now, Mr Doyle, you're in hut number ten, which is close to our new pool. You've arrived on the right day. The infinity pool was only opened this morning. I dipped my toe in and it's lovely and warm. There are beach towels in your hut if you'd like a swim.'

'Thank you.' Ronan pulled his handkerchief from his pocket and dabbed at his forehead. It was stifling hot on the island. 'I think that's the first thing I'll do.'

'Make sure you read your compendium and take heed of the warnings about stingers and crocodiles in the ocean. We may be in paradise here, but you still have to be careful.'

'I will.'

'We'll bring your suitcase to your hut once they're offloaded from the launch. I hope you have an enjoyable stay with us, and don't hesitate to ask if there's anything you need.'

Ronan nodded and lifted his laptop case from where he'd rested it on the floor to check in. 'One question, Tess. Wi-Fi?'

She nodded and as she spoke the door opened behind them. 'Yes, all the details are in the compendium in your room. If you require extra data or any assistance, our two IT guys live on the island after hours. Just leave a message at reception, and either Nat or Gabe will get back to you.'

'Thank—'

'Oh my goodness, it's as sweet inside as out. Look at those gorgeous curtains. Oh my God, and the view.'

Ronan froze as the Irish accent filled the small space. He flashed a smile at Tess, nodded and hurried from reception, hoping that the receptionist wouldn't comment about an Irishman being in the resort. Walking away quickly, he followed the signs directing him through a small rainforest to the huts. He was pleasantly surprised by the absolute quiet that surrounded him. If he had to be here working, it was certainly one of the nicer places he'd been to during the past three years. Once this assignment was over, he was going back home to retire from investigative work. If he'd finally tracked down his quarry—and he was pretty sure he had— the bonus alone would be enough to allow him to buy into his brother-in-law's commercial photography business in Dublin.

Ronan shrugged off the thought that working in the one location every day would be dull. Being in one room working with digital images could possibly be boring after his work travels of the past few years. He'd just have to get used to it. Granted, Patrick had contracts with some of the biggest firms in the UK and he still worked with film for some of the more detailed jobs, but strangely the thought of being back in the industry Ronan had worked in for ten years before moving into this present work didn't excite him anymore.

A bird squawked in the spreading tree above and Ronan lifted his face to the sun as he stepped out of the rainforest. Following the sign to hut ten, he thought about going back to the cold and grey of Dublin in winter. Living somewhere like this was much more appealing.

He'd been unsettled since Briony had dumped him a couple of years back.

'Boring, Ronan. All you think about is your job and a pint at the pub on Friday nights. I don't want my life to be like that. He'd had a rethink, and realised she was right. Taking on the investigative work had given him the opportunity to see the world outside of Dingle. Problem was, now that he had, he didn't know if he could face going back.

Ronan pulled his thoughts back to the present. He couldn't afford to lose focus. This assignment was a delicate one; when he'd lost his target before, he had begun to doubt his ability and worry that he'd lost his edge. This time he'd take it slow and carefully; if it took a few weeks to achieve his goal, so be it. Apparently, she'd taken a job here.

He'd booked the hut for a month to give himself plenty of time to set the trap.

Forget home and the future. The best thing was, he was on a tropical island, in a beautiful location, the weather was hot and clear—no misty rain that chilled you to the bone here. Maybe he should consider emigrating. Ronan frowned as he put the key in the door of hut ten; the door opened smoothly, and he stepped inside.

Where had that thought come from?

He looked around the room and let out a contented sigh. A floor to ceiling window provided an uninterrupted view of sapphire-blue water, and the gentle breeze ruffled the fronds of two palm trees framing the scene.

Maybe the idea wasn't so foolish after all. He had the skills to take up a few different careers. Maybe later, he'd open his laptop and see what was available in North Queensland.

Ronan put his laptop case on the luggage rack and slipped his shoes off. The white tiles were cool beneath his feet as he crossed the spacious room to the window. For what was classed as a hut, the room was pretty impressive. A king-size bed sat beneath the window with two white towels in a roll on the white coverlet. A posy of yellow and white flowers sat on top of the towels.

Wasted on a single guy here for work, he thought, but he appreciated the romantic touch. Leaning forward a little, he looked through the window. To the left he could just see the edge of the swimming pool the receptionist had mentioned. Past the pool was an expanse of water, broken only by the white sail of a lone yacht. To the right, a hut identical to his sat at the end of a short white stone path edged with colourful flowers.

Paradise, to be sure.

The only noise was the soft swish of the cane blades of the fan above and the low hum of the refrigerator in the small kitchenette in the corner. Ronan walked across to the door at the end of the kitchen counter, and opened it, peering inside at a compact bathroom tiled in white from floor to ceiling

Relaxation seeped through him. He'd keep a low profile today, maybe have a swim, boot up his laptop, email his client and do some more research on the life and movements of the O'Sullivan woman. Sometime in the next day or so he'd try to get a photo of her and send it to his client.

Chapter Five
Dublin. Ten years earlier.

'Aisling, I don't know if I want to go down there.' Celia grabbed her arm as Aisling turned into a back street three blocks from *Sanity.* 'It looks a bit dodgy.'

'It's fine. Robbie in the music store said there's a tattoo parlour down here who'll do the first small tat for free.'

Celia drew her breath in and her gasp annoyed Aisling. 'Jesus, Celia, what's wrong now?'

'A tat? That's permanent.'

'So?' Aisling stopped walking and stared at her friend. 'You don't have to get one. You can watch while I get mine.'

'You're going to get a tattoo? What will your parents say?'

'They won't see it.'

Another gasp. 'Where?'

'On my butt. A butterfly. I saw one on TV the other night. It looked friggin' cool.'

Aisling looked down the street and she knew Celia was right; it was the dodgy end of the city but she wasn't going to let Celia see her hesitate. Two homeless guys lounged in a doorway, one covered with a ragged coat, the other staring at them as he sat on the doorstep sucking on a cigarette. A shopping trolley filled with their possessions lay on an angle in the gutter. On the opposite side of the street, a young guy with a pock-marked face leaned on the bonnet of an old, rusted car watching them.

Aisling wrapped her black coat around her; the wind whistling down the street was fecking freezing. 'There's the tattoo shop down there. Are you going to come with me or wimp out?'

'I guess I'll come with you. I'm not walking back by myself. But I'm not going to watch. I'd spew.'

'Suit yourself.' Aisling took off, stepping onto the road as she passed the old guys and flicking a finger at the young guy as he yelled out to them.

'Wanna have some fun, ladies? I can handle two of you at once.'

'In your dreams, boyo,' Aisling yelled back, but she picked up the pace, they'd already spent two hours wandering around the shops. 'Come on Celia, we haven't got all day.'

##

'Bloody Nora, that hurts.'

'Just lie still, love. I'm almost done.' The tattoo guy paused for a few seconds before starting to ink her again. Aisling bit her lip. It would be worth it.

It would. Another sign of rebellion; even if they didn't see it, she'd know it was there.

In the end, Celia had decided to come in and watch; Aisling knew it was because she was too scared to sit out in the waiting room by herself.

'It's really pretty, Ash.' Celia sounded surprised.

'Are you going to get one too, lovey?'

'Oh, no. My parents'd kill me.'

'They don't have to see it.'

Her friend shook her head. 'No. I don't want to.'

'Whatever.'

A few minutes later the tattooist straightened. 'You're done, love. You want to see it?'

'Of course I bloody do.'

He shrugged and walked away and picked up two round mirrors from the cluttered bench. Handing her one, he moved to her side and held the other mirror above her backside. Aisling propped herself up on her elbows and adjusted the angle of the mirror, and nodded. 'It's cool. Thanks.'

With a shrug, he took the mirror from her. 'Ten quid, love.'

'I thought the first one was free.'

'In your dreams. A man has to make a living. Come out when you're dressed.'

As soon as the door closed, Celia widened her eyes and whispered. 'Ten pounds! Didn't you spend all your money at *Sanity?*'

Aisling slipped off the bench and pulled her black jeans up over the new tat. She grimaced as the fabric touched her tender skin. 'Nuh, I slipped those CDs into my coat.'

Celia stared at her and then giggled. 'Gosh, you're bad, Ash. But I love it.'

'Bad?' Aisling buttoned up her coat. 'Stick with me, kid. You ain't seen nothing yet.'

Bad? she thought to herself. Sometimes it was all too hard, but it was the only payback Aisling knew. Some nights she lay there in bed dreaming of being in a normal family where there were happy people and love. Not this constant pressure to perform, and turn into a clone of her parents and her sister.

Bloody Marlene had enrolled in her law degree, and Da had the same plans for Aisling. To come into the family law firm: O'Sullivan and O'Sullivan. Mam and Da, woops Mother and Father, were both solicitors. Aisling grinned, wondering whether it would be called O'Sullivan, O'Sullivan and O'Sullivan when Marlene joined them. It certainly wouldn't be any longer because she had no intention of doing law.

'I know you've still got a few months before your university entrance exams, but you cannot afford to fail one thing, Aisling,' he'd said when she failed her exam. 'You can spend the next two weeks in your room brushing up on your mathematics.'

There was no need to do that. She would have been able to blitz that exam if she'd wanted, but rebellion had kicked in when her mother had told her the morning of the exam that she'd booked her in for a beauty treatment for the coming weekend.

'No. I'm going to a rock concert with Celia this weekend.'

'No, Aisling. Your hair and eyebrows need attention, and I saw a pimple on your face yesterday.'

'I squeezed it.'

She might as well as said she'd murdered someone by the look on Mam's face.

'All the more reason to have a facial treatment. I'll talk to Celia's mother and pay for Celia to go with you for the weekend.'

'No. If I have to go to the stupid place, I'll go by myself. Anyway, Mrs Donohue would be embarrassed if you said that. There's no need to flaunt how rich you are, *Mam*.'

'Mother.'

'Bloody hell,' Aisling said. *'Mother.'*

She turned to Celia as they stepped out of the tattoo parlour. 'Come on, I need a drink.'

Chapter Six
Pippa

The Friday after Isla arrived on the island, I was late getting down to our regular sunset drinks on the shore. Eliza and I had an afternoon meeting with Renzo and Danny Riccardo, getting ready for the handover of the staff lodge. We'd toured the building, checked out the final tiling jobs in each of the ensuites, and looked over the large kitchen and other communal areas. All that was waiting was the new furniture for each room arriving by barge early next week. Ten single rooms ran along the western side of the building looking over the island, and five doubles, to cater for couples who worked on the island, both now and in the future, overlooked the water. A wide verandah facing north provided an outdoor relaxation area, and a barbeque.

I turned to Eliza with a huge grin. 'They are going to love this.'

'I can't get over how spacious the rooms are. Bigger than our cabin on Phillipe's boat.' She pulled a face.

'You're quite welcome to take one of the doubles, you know.'

'Don't tempt me.'

Tamsin and Gabe, and Nat and Nell were going to move into two of the double suites while their houses were being built. Angus and Cherry were moving across too. Odessa and Dylan had asked to stay in the building behind the old house close to where she had set up her jewellery making studio. Having the single rooms meant that we could have kitchen hands and housemaids living at the resort now rather than having to come across on the launch each day. Sienna and Isla would take a single room each.

'Absolutely fantastic, guys. Love, love, love it.' I turned back to Eliza. 'You did a great job with the colour scheme.'

Muted blues and greens in the bedrooms replicated the hues of the sea and forest, and the communal rooms: kitchen, games room and living room were painted white, with charcoal benchtops in the kitchen.

'I'm 'ere to please,' she said with a grin, putting on her Cockney accent. I'd smothered a grin a few times lately. Eliza put on a stronger accent and dropped her aitches in front of Odessa to get a rise out of her, and Odessa took the bait every time. Mind you, Odessa put on her plummy tones to stir Eliza too.

Renzo shook his head and held his hands up. 'You should be using this building for guests. Too good for workers.'

I shook my head. 'We look after our staff.'

'And they love you,' Danny chimed in with a smile.

'It's so good, I'll talk to Phillipe,' Eliza said. 'I could live here.'

'You'll never get him off his boat, sweets,' I said with a grin.

'I know. Just as well I like living on the water.' Eliza looked down at her phone. 'We're late for sunset drinks, Pip. I'm happy to sign off, are you?'

'I am. Great job, guys. Thank you.'

'Okay,' Renzo said. 'We'll get the last of the building gear out of here tomorrow, get the furniture in place on Monday, and your lucky staff should be right to move up around Tuesday.'

'Excellent. And then you will start on Aunty Vi's house?'

'Yes, we're ready to keep going.'

Eliza and I walked down the hill and she flicked a glance at me. 'Why the frown?'

'You know me. I always worry when things go too well. It's like tempting fate.'

A loud voice and laughter drifted across as we approached the beach. Isla was holding court and stood in the centre of the group with her hands on her hips. 'And Paulie told Ma he wanted to have ten kids, and Ma told him off. "Think of your poor wife, boy," she said. We all laughed but it was seeing Ma chasing him down the path with a broom that set us all off.'

I rolled my eyes and Eliza caught me.

'Not happy?'

'She's got an over the top personality.'

'She seems to be keeping everyone entertained.'

'Maybe I'm turning into an old cranky pants.'

Eliza chuckled and shook her head. 'We're getting older.'

As we got closer, Sienna interrupted Isla, the teller of the tale. Her musical accent was soft after the Irish brogue. 'But tell us, why would she chase him with the broom? I do not understand.'

'She always did with Paulie. He was always the naughtiest when we were growing up.'

Cherry's smile was wistful. 'I envy your big family. It sounds like a happy family despite the broom!'

'Oh, we were when we were growing up, and now with all the grandchildren, it's starting all over again.'

'How many grandchildren?' Nell asked.

'Oh, I do lose track,' Isla said. 'Let me see.' She counted off on her fingers. 'Paulie has Morag, and Johnnie, Johnnie has Susie and Paulie, Archie has Ian and Aisling, and Barrie's wife, Jennifer is expecting their first. So that makes almost seven'

'What about your other brother?' Sienna asked.

Isla shook her head. 'I only have four brothers.'

'I thought you had five?'

'No, thank goodness. Only four.' Isla looked away from Sienna.

'Do you miss them?' Nell asked as Eliza and I settled on a rock. Cherry poured two glasses of champagne and handed them to us.

'Thanks, love,' Eliza said as we clinked the glasses.

'Bloody hell, no. Screaming whinging kids. I had enough of that growing up in our tiny house. We Facetime once a month when they all go home for Sunday lunch. That's enough for me!' Isla looked across to Eliza and I. 'Hello, there, you pair. I love this idea of sunset drinks, Pippa.'

'It's a good way to wind down,' I said quietly. It was interesting to see the change in dynamic down here on the beach. We usually had a few quiet conversations going, but tonight Isla was centre stage; she was a very charismatic person. I wondered how she was going in the day spa. If she was so vocal with her clients, it might be a bit off-putting. I'd check in with Sienna later.

I sipped my champagne and enjoyed the fizz of the bubbles on my tongue. Isla was still holding court, talking about her primary school days in a place called Dingle. I shook off the annoyance that surfaced briefly. As Isla kept speaking to her seemingly spellbound audience, Sienna stood and moved across to stand at the edge of the water. I rose and followed her.

She turned to me with a smile, but I had seen the frown before I approached. 'Hi Pippa, have you had a good day?'

'I have. How about you?'

'Busy. We've been fully booked all week since Isla arrived.' Her glance swivelled back to the rocks where the rest of the girls were sitting.

'How's Isla fitting in?'

Sienna nodded slowly. 'Really well. In the treatment rooms, she is quiet and professional, and the feedback from the guests who have seen her this week has been excellent.'

'But?' I prompted.

Her delicate arched eyebrows rose as she turned to look at me. 'But what?'

'I sense some hesitation there.' I lowered my voice. 'As you know, each staff member comes on a one-month probation period. If you don't think she's going to work out, you need to let me know.'

Sienna's fair skin coloured slightly. 'Oh no, it's nothing like that. I've just been tired this week, and sharing a room with Isla has been—shall I say— a *leetle* bit full on. But please ignore me. I'm used to my quiet time at night, and I just have to get used to sharing a room.'

'That's fine, but if you have any issues, you make sure you let me know. Friendship can't get in the way of us having the best staff on Pentecost Island. And the good news is, that the staff lodge is ready, and you'll probably be able to move up in a few days. Eliza and I just gave it the tick of approval. The Riccardo boys have done an excellent job.'

'Danny is a very talented builder. He's shown me some of their projects on Hamilton Island.'

'You both look very happy together. How's it all going?'

'We are, and things are moving well. The solicitor who is helping Danny to leave his marriage has made excellent progress.'

'That's good news.'

Sienna and Danny had had a rocky start to their relationship, but it had all been resolved on another island when she had gone away to do some training. Coincidentally, Isla had been at the training course at the upmarket resort on Esculanta Island and her employment with us had come from their meeting there.

Another burst of laughter came from the group, and I stood. 'I'll go and let everyone know that the move up the hill is imminent.'

An hour later, I walked back to the old house with Tamsin and Nell. Tamsin had been quiet on the shore, and I had a feeling that she wasn't too impressed with Isla either. When we stepped out of the glade and approached the house, I paused.

'So, what do you think of Isla?'

Nell chuckled. 'She's like a breath of fresh air. I love that accent.'

'Tam?'

Tamsin put one hand to her back, and I frowned.

'You were quiet over there,' I said. 'You're not impressed?'

'I didn't take much notice.' Tam's voice was quiet and strained. 'I'm actually not feeling very good.'

Nell and I moved quickly across the path to her side.

'What's wrong?' Nell asked urgently as Tamsin grabbed at our hands as her knees buckled under her.

'I have a pain in my back, and I think I'm going to faint.' Her face lost all its colour and Nell and I supported her across to the steps, and sat her down on the bottom one, and she put her head between her knees.

'Can you call Gabe, please. He's still over on Hamo.' Her breath sounded short. 'He and Nat had a late job there.'

I nodded and made sure that Nell was right with Tamsin before I hurried into the office. This was the only downside to being on our island.

Medical emergencies.

Tess had stayed in the office tonight; she'd insisted on staying back and doing the end of week run, as she and Zac were going cruising south to the Shaw group of islands for the weekend.

'Tess, can you please look up the number for Prossie hospital for me, and get them on the line. Tam's not well.' She heard the urgency in my request and typed into her keyboard immediately. Luckily, I had Gabe's number in my phone and I pressed speed dial.

He picked up immediately. 'Pippa?'

'Gabe, don't panic, but Tamsin's not feeling very well.'

'God, is the baby coming? It's way too early.'

'No, at least I don't think so.' I knew nothing about babies and birth, apart from the pain and distress of my recent miscarriage. 'She's a bit lightheaded and her back's hurting. I'm just going to ring the hospital and see what they say. I think the medical centre on Hamo will be closed by now.'

'I'm on my way. I'll swing by the centre and see if anyone's still there on the way to the marina.'

'Do that but wait a short while before you come back. Depending on what the hospital says, we might bring her straight over to Hamo on Rafe's boat. I'll call you straight back after I talk to them. Do you have Nell's number? Give her a call. She's out there with Tam now. You can talk to Tam.'

'No, I don't, but Nat's here. I'll get the number off him.'

'Okay, I'll call you back in five.'

I was worried and on edge as Tess passed me the office mobile. I'd jinxed Tam by worrying that something was going to happen when I'd said that everything was going too well. 'Can you call Rafe and get him down here too, please Tess.'

My call to Proserpine Hospital was brief.

Chapter Seven

Aisling

Dublin. Ten years earlier.

Aisling took pity on Celia, and they walked three blocks before she found a likely looking bar. One that Celia would be comfortable in. Sometimes, Aisling wondered how they had stayed friends. She gestured with a short jerk of her head, and Celia followed her into the dark pub without a word.

A group of elderly men sitting at a table in the corner were the only other patrons, but an appetising aroma drifted out from the kitchen, masking the stale smell of beer and smoke. Aisling pulled out her phone and checked the time, ignoring three text message notifications from her mother.

Shit, obviously sprung. Bloody Marlene.

She pulled a face.

'What's wrong?' Celia's voice held its usual lack of confidence and Aisling wondered why she had even asked her to come to the city with her.

'Nothing.' She rolled her eyes. 'It's almost one. Drink, then food. I'll go and get a menu; you grab that table. What do you want to drink?'

'Ginger ale, please.'

As always, Celia did as Aisling instructed. With a shrug she waited until Celia was sitting at the table in the far corner, and she headed to the bar.

The barman had his back to her washing glasses, and she waited for him to turn around.

When he finally turned and put the cloth on the bar, Aisling drew a breath.

Mother of God, he was a fine thing. She was in instant lust.

She fluttered her mascara-enhanced lashes at him and smiled. 'Hello.'

'Good morning, lovely. What can I get you?' Deep blue eyes surrounded by lush—unenhanced—lashes sat in a beautiful face. Pale white skin, high cheekbones and a lock of dark hair falling across a high brow got her attention. A slow and sexy smile tilted his lips as he retuned her gaze. He looked just like she imagined Dylan Thomas would have looked.

She adored his poetry, and when things were really bad at home, she'd lie on her bed with her earphones blocking out any interruptions and listen to Dylan Thomas reading his poetry.

The only thing this guy didn't have was the Welsh accent, but Aisling was in instant love. She'd been going to order an ale for herself, but suddenly it didn't seem sophisticated enough.

'I'll have a glass of white wine, please, and a ginger ale for my friend.'

He didn't move and held her eyes with his for what seemed like minutes. Heat filled her cheeks as he kept staring.

'You don't remember me, do you?' he finally said.

'Remember you?' Her voice was breathless. 'Should I?'

'I was two years above you at Castleknock College.'

'Oh.' Aisling narrowed her eyes and stared at him. 'I don't remember you.'

Was it a pick-up line or was he for real? She was smitten, but smart enough to be careful.

'I always thought what a pretty little thing you were, but you've grown up. And you've obviously spread your wings. Have you left school?'

A pretty little thing? Okay, could be better, but she could live with that.

What to say?

'I'm thinking about it.' That was vague enough.

Reaching across to the shelf he took down a bottle of wine and opened it. 'Half or full?' Those glorious eyes met hers as he held the glass up.

'Full please.'

His voice was deep and melodious, and a memory tugged as he stared at her.

'Oh my love is like a red, red rose

That's newly sprung in June;

So fair art thou, my bonnie lass,

So deep in love am I,' he recited in that sexy voice. The penny dropped.

'You spoke at the school assembly when Mr Laidlaw died, didn't you? I do remember you now. You read a poem you'd written about him.'

'Ah, thank you, God. She remembers me.' He put one hand to his chest as he poured the wine.

'I remember your voice, and I always remembered those beautiful words you wrote about him. I loved Mr Laidlaw.' Guilt trickled through Aisling as she thought what that fine teacher would have said about her bunking off from school, and her lack of ambition, if he'd still been alive.

'He was a brilliant teacher, and he inspired me to keep writing poetry.' He filled the glass and took a small bottle of ginger ale from the shelf.

'And you were in that student production of *Under Milkwood*. You played Captain Cat.'

'Ah, she remembers more.'

'I remember your voice, but I can't remember your name.'

'Now I'm heartbroken. Never once did I forget your pretty face, Rose Red, and *you* don't even recall my name.'

'What's your name?'

'Niall Buckley. I'm very pleased you remember me though, if not my name.' His dark eyes stayed on hers. 'Perhaps we could have a drink when I finish work and raise a glass to Mr Laidlaw? How long will you be in town for?'

'Long enough. I'd like that.' Aisling could have drowned in those eyes, and that voice, *oh my freakin' God.* 'I'd like that very much.'

##

Aisling and Celia rode the bus home from the city so that they'd arrive in Castleknock at the normal end of school time. For Celia's benefit that was; it didn't matter when Aisling got home because her parents would have some dinner or meeting in the city. She wondered why they bothered living out at Castleknock when they could have had an apartment in town close to the office.

As the bus headed the eight kilometres out of town, she found it hard to keep still. As she wriggled on the seat, the tender skin on her backside reminded her of the tattoo. Her head had been so full of Niall, and the meeting they'd planned, she'd totally forgotten about her act of rebellion, but now the tenderness of her skin reminded her. It had been important to her at the start of the day, but once she'd met Niall, she'd not even thought of it.

She'd said not a word to Celia about him, and when she'd put their drinks on the table, Celia had been intent on her phone and obviously hadn't noticed her chatting.

As they'd sat there in the dark corner Aisling had taken a hefty sip of her wine and pulled her phone out to look at the messages from her mother, trying not to return her gaze to the bar. She knew he was looking at her, she could feel the pull of Niall's gaze from across the room.

She dropped her eyes to her phone.

Shite. Sprung.

Why aren't you at school? Where are you? Your father is livid. AND I mean LIVID. Sister Mary rang.

Aisling grinned as she typed the reply. She would show them she didn't care. What could they do?

I had better things to do today than listen to Sister Mary rave on about geography. I'll be home late.

Hopefully very late, she thought an hour later after she'd left Celia at the bus stop and then walked around the corner to catch the bus back into town. She wasn't prepared to take the risk of going home to freshen up, in case her mother had gone home to wait for her.

Pigs might fly too. She'd go into the restroom at the railway station and redo her makeup.

Niall was knocking off at five and they were meeting at another bar in the city.

I can't be all bad, Aisling thought. *I saw Celia home safely.* A twinge of guilt tugged at her and for a brief second, she wondered if she should go home and face the music.

No, the appeal of spending time with a boy—a man—who quoted poetry to her and called her Rose Red, was much more enticing than the prospect of confronting her father. Maybe it was time to think about getting a job and leaving home. Leaving school. The last thing she wanted was to go to university.

Aisling knew she was smart enough, but the thought of following in her parents' and her sister's footsteps filled her with dread. Maybe she could get a job in a bar. Her excitement built as she stepped off the bus in Marlborough Street. Her hands were clammy, and there was an unfamiliar warm and hollow feeling in her chest. Anticipation built as she looked around. A smile tugged as she spotted Niall leaning against the sun-drenched building beside *The Confession Box* bar.

So much for freshening up.

He held a small book in one hand, and she could see his lips moving as he read the words. The last rays of the setting sun highlighted blue lights in his black hair. Aisling shivered as that strange feeling spread through her. A feeling that this man was going to be a part of her life. There was no need to put on her tough act; she could be herself with Niall. Maybe even she could be the pretty little thing he remembered.

But did she want to take that step towards him? The strong feeling that consumed her made her hesitate. This man would change her life; she was as sure of that as she was that the sun was going to drop over Killiney Hill in half an hour.

She took a step towards him, and then hesitated, but he must have caught her movement from the corner of his eye, or maybe he simply sensed her presence.

Slowly, Niall lifted his head, and when their eyes connected, Aisling stepped towards him.

No hesitation, no doubt. This was her path. This was where she wanted to be.

If it was a different path to that of her parents, then that's the way it would be.

She walked over to him, her confidence growing with each step. It might be too fast, but, she was sure.

A smile spread over his face as she reached him, and his eyes stayed on hers.

'I knew you'd come.' Niall leaned forward and took her hand, moving closer. Aisling held her breath as he lowered his head to hers and his whisper warmed her cheek.

'Shall I compare thee to a summer's day? Thou art more lovely . . . '

Chapter Eight
Ronan

The magic of being on a tropical island in the Down Under summer, when he knew it would be bleak and sleeting at home in Dublin, buoyed Ronan's spirits. As did his certainty that he was on the right track and that he had finally hit pay dirt. He was sure the new beauty therapist on the island was indeed the woman he'd been searching for over the past year. O'Sullivan was a common surname, but the photo he'd taken of her from the top of the hill with his telephoto lens this morning which he'd sent to his client had come back with an affirmative.

This was the closest and the longest he had been near her, and Ronan had managed to get a clear headshot when he'd been up on the track above the resort under the pretext of bird watching. He'd sent the photo to his client and had had a reply within minutes.

Yes, that is my sister.

The confirmation from Ireland that he had finally found the O'Sullivan woman was the easy part. The second part of his assignment—to get her back to Dublin—was going to be way more problematic. At least being on an island with only two ferries a day arriving and departing, meant he could keep a closer eye on her. With any luck she couldn't disappear into the night. He wondered if that was why he had lost her before, that she had been aware of him looking for her.

As he walked along the beach at sunset on his fifth day on the island, he considered the various ways he could go about it.

His first option was to tell her exactly what was going on and hope that she would be reasonable and listen to him. Ronan shook his head. Anyone who'd covered their tracks for so long didn't want to be found, and certainly wasn't going to listen to him and follow him happily back to Dublin.

Second option? Find out why she was hiding and try to find a way that might convince her that she needed to go home. Show some empathy and get her to trust him. Again, it was clear that she didn't want to be found, and she wasn't going to trust a stranger with her deep secrets. The whole assignment was top secret, and apart from a few details, he'd been employed to find her and bring her back to Ireland. There had been some mention of an inheritance, and that the woman was required to attend a solicitor's office in person. He got the impression there was a large amount of money involved.

Third option? There wasn't one, apart from kidnapping her. Until he got to know her and made a judgment call on her likely response, Ronan knew he was working in the dark.

As he looked away from the water, a movement over towards the huts caught his attention. The beauty therapist with the red hair walked down the steps of the day spa towards the path and then disappeared into the forest. There was no sign of the Irish one, but a light was glowing from the hut,

Ronan narrowed his eyes; he'd kept a low profile on the island, hadn't got into any conversations with other guests or the staff, apart from the occasional please and thank you. He'd been totally focused on trying to figure out what to do, now that he'd found her.

A glimmer of light shone from the back window as another light was switched on. She was still in there.

Alone.

An idea formed and Ronan quickened his pace as he walked towards the day spa.

Chapter Nine
Isla

Isla had sensed a couple of days ago that Sienna needed space. They'd both had a day of back-to-back appointments, and when the last client left Sienna flopped into the chair behind the reception counter

'Oh my goodness, what a busy day that was. I'm so pleased that you're here now, Isla. Pippa and Eliza will be very pleased with the business we've done today. It's a record day for *Hebe*.' She put her head back and rested one hand on her forehead and Isla wondered how Sienna managed to look fresh and cool after such a busy day.

Isla reached up and tucked her hair up beneath the white bandanna. Her curls had come loose, as they always did, and she knew her makeup had run in the heat today. 'Yes, all of my clients went for the top of the range package. One of the women said she'd heard about us down in Sydney.' Isla sat in the cane chair by the window where the clients waited.

'Yes, the word is really spreading about Pentecost Island, and about *Hebe*. I am very pleased to be here,' Sienna said. 'Are you liking it here already? Do you think you will stay for a while before you move on?'

Isla put her head back and rested it against the smooth timber wall. 'I'll be honest with you. I'm sorry I've been so social this week. I know I've been a bit tiring for you.'

'No, no, not at all. It is a pleasure to have you here.'

'Come on, lovely, be honest. I think you are pleased that we now have our own rooms.'

'Okay. Well maybe just a little bit. I do like my own company.'

'I can't help being how I am. I guess it covers up what I'm lacking.'

'Lacking? What do you mean?'

Isla shrugged. She'd said too much already. This island was working its spell on her, and she was relaxing her guard. She knew she'd already slipped up the other night when she'd accidentally forgotten one of her "brothers", and Sienna had picked up on it.

'I guess I blather on and run away at the mouth so—'

'So that you are liked by new friends?' Sienna's voice was soft. 'I like you, Isla and I know the others do too. You have fitted in already, but I will say that there is no need to try so hard. You are a good person.'

Isla's eyes stung as tears threatened; she blinked. For the first time in five years of travelling, she'd found somewhere she'd like to stay. A beautiful island where she had good employment with fabulous pay, a great room, and—for a change—other women close by, who she was sure she could become friends with.

Women, she sensed, she could trust and who would back her if she needed support.

She cleared her throat. 'Thank you, Sienna. That means a lot to me. More than you can ever know. And that's all I'm saying.' She jumped to her feet. 'Now lovely, I know that gorgeous man of yours will be waiting to see you before he goes back to his island, so get yourself over to the bar. I'll put the towels in the machine and have a tidy up. We've got another busy day tomorrow. You're fully booked, and I have one space first thing.'

Sienna stood slowly and stretched. 'Thank you, I'll accept that very kind offer. Don't worry too much, we can tidy up in the morning.'

'No, I'll be happy to potter around here for an hour or so while the towels dry. You go, and I'll be over to the kitchen for dinner in a while.'

Sienna shook her head. 'I think we should celebrate tonight. Danny has to go back to Hamo after I see him. He's flying to Port Douglas tomorrow for a meeting with his solicitor. I think you and I should have dinner at the restaurant—if they can fit us in.'

'That would be grand,' Isla said. 'I'd like that very much. So, shoo. Go and see your man, and I'll tidy up here. I feel manky; I need a shower before dinner. I'll see you in a while.'

After Sienna left, Isla changed the music on the iPod to something more upbeat than soothing rainforest bird calls and muted music. She gathered up the used towels and facecloths from both treatment rooms and took them to the compact laundry at the back of the hut. Starting the hot wash cycle, she added a capful of bleach to the machine, and set it for a quick wash. As she topped up products from the storage cupboard in the hall between the two rooms, she hummed along with the music. Now that she was here, she'd ease back on the loud and extroverted personality. She'd been accepted by the staff, and apart from clients in *Hebe*, she'd keep herself separate from the guests.

Most clients preferred peace and quiet while they had their treatments, not someone blathering away in an Irish accent. Isla had watched how calm and focused Sienna was as she worked and knew she would take a leaf out of her book.

Picking up the spray bottle and a clean cloth, she walked into the reception area, singing along with the Corrs *Summer Sunshine* and trying not to let the lyrics make her sad. That part of her life was over.

She'd moved on.

Isla leaned down behind the counter and wiped down the shelves.

'Hello.'

She jumped as the screen door clicked shut and a tall man filled the doorway.

'I wasn't sure if you were still open.' The voice with a strong Irish accent had her heart rate leaping.

'We're done for the day,' she said softy, as she put the bottle and cloth on the floor behind the counter. 'What can I do for you?'

As she stood, she looked up into a serious face, a frown marring a broad forehead.

'Ah, I'm sorry to come after hours, but Nell in reception said it might be best if I came here to make an appointment direct.' He gestured to the mobile on the counter. 'She did try to call, but there was no answer, and she thought you might both still be busy.'

Isla picked up the phone and checked it. 'Ah, it was still on mute.'

He nodded without speaking as she flicked off the mute button on the side of the mobile.

'Is the appointment for you? Or—'

'Yes, it is for me.' His face coloured as she looked back at him. The poor guy looked very much out of place in a day spa.

'I . . . ah . . . I feel like an eejit. I slipped on some loose rocks when I was walking this morning and I noticed in the compendium you do a hot stone massage, and ah,'— he cleared his throat—'do you have any free appointments tomorrow?'

'You're in luck. I do have one open at eight thirty tomorrow morning. Is that too early?'

'Oh, no not at all. I'm usually up walking a couple of hours before that.' He lifted his hand and for the first time she noticed he was holding a camera with a huge telephoto lens. 'I'm a nature photographer. And early morning is the best time to come across creatures feeding, and with brilliant light too.'

His cheeks were pink as she stared back at him, and Isla wondered if it was due to his fair complexion, or embarrassment at being in a day spa.

'Where did you hurt? Your back?'

He nodded and gestured to his lower back. 'Ay. It's not too bad, but I can't afford to miss the early start to the day, and I think I might come up sore tomorrow.'

Isla opened the booking screen on the laptop. 'I'll book you in for eight-thirty then. For a hot stone massage?'

'Yes, please.'

She hesitated and then looked up at him again. He was staring at her, and it made her feel uncomfortable.

'Your name, sir?'

'Oh, sorry. My name is Ronan Doyle.'

Chapter Ten
Pippa

I was walking past the office on my way to the new staff building when Nell ran out of the office holding the phone.

'Whoa, slow down, or you'll be over on the mainland in the hospital with Tam.'

Nell's grin was wide, and she shoved the office phone at me. 'Tam's on the phone. She has news.'

'Everything okay?' I said, taking the phone. 'She was good when I talked to her last night.'

'She's coming home. Gabe's with her now and they're catching the eleven o'clock ferry back from the mainland to Hamo.'

'Great. I'll send Rafe over to pick them up.' I took the phone and Nell stood there still grinning as I answered.

'Hey, Tamsin. Great news Nell tells me.'

Nell was clapping her hands and jumping around.

'What did she tell you?' Tam's voice was as dry as ever. She'd been in the hospital on the mainland while they ran some tests, and up until last night, everything had come back fine. I'd not been as worried as I had been a few days earlier when she'd been taken ill, because she was in the right place, and at six months along, all the tests had come back as they should. Her self-diagnosis was that she was simply overtired from doing too much, and the doctors had agreed with her.

'That you're on your way home today. And when you're home, you're going to put your feet up and knit baby booties. No more helping out in the restaurant or running up the hill to look at your block of land.'

'Yes, Mum,' she said with a chuckle. 'Are you quite finished?'

'I am. We'll see you later. I'll send Rafe over to Hamo.'

'Phillipa!' I could hear the exasperation in your voice. 'Will you listen to me. I have some news. I had another scan.'

'And you know now if you need pink or blue booties?' I grinned at Nell. She was still squirming with excitement. 'By the look on Nell's face, I'd say it's a girl.'

Nell rolled her eyes and mouthed at me. 'Listen to Tamsin!'

'I do know,' Tam said. 'And I think you'll need to get your knitting needles out too.'

'I can't knit,' I said. 'Hang on a minute.' I turned to Nell. 'Are you okay. Do you need the loo?'

Nell folded her arms and gestured to the phone. 'Listen!'

With a shrug, I turned back to the call. 'Nell told me to listen to you.'

'I've been waiting. What I want to tell you is that we need both pink and blue booties.' Tamsin's voice broke as my mouth dropped open. 'We're having twins. A boy and a girl.'

'Oh my God.' I stood there as Nell flung her arms around me.

'Twins!' she squealed. 'We're going to have three babies on the island.' Nell grabbed the phone from me. 'Celebration tonight? Or are you too tired?'

I stood there, feeling happy for Tam and Gabe, and surprised that my sadness stayed away as I processed the news.

Life on our island was going to change this year.

##

It didn't take long for Tam and Gabe's news to spread through the staff, and when Rafe and I sat in *Violet's*, our main restaurant, with Nell and Nat, and Tam and Gabe that evening, there was a constant stream of friends stopping at the table to say congratulations.

Rafe held my hand under the table, and the occasional squeeze of his fingers soothed me, and kept me smiling.

At one stage Cherry came out of the kitchen, with a small bunch of pink and blue balloons and tied them to the back of Tam's chair.

'Where on earth did you find them?' I asked.

'We are prepared for any occasion in *Violet's* restaurant,' she said. Leaning down to brush a kiss on Tam's cheek, Cherry caught my eye. 'Angus has excelled himself tonight. He's put on a special menu for this table. You're not allowed to order, he said.'

'Angus excels himself every night,' Rafe said with a nod.

'He does, 'I agreed. 'We'll wait to see what he's created for us tonight.'

When Cherry had gone back into the kitchen, Tam sat back in her chair and placed her hands on top of her large stomach. She'd grown bigger in the week she'd been away. She must have read my thoughts because she nodded. 'And I'm going to get way bigger than this by June.'

It was a happy night, with lots of soda water consumed by the girls, and Angus did excel himself with a new beef dish that he'd created.

I hugged Tam as we said goodnight, but I frowned as I looked up the hill to the staff lodge. 'Are you right to walk up there?'

'I have to be,' she said. 'But yes. If I take it easy, I'll be fine.'

I was thoughtful as Rafe and I climbed up the steps to our house on the hill.

'Okay, love?' he said putting his arm around me.

'I am. I'm happy for them. Both of them. Tamsin and Nell. I wasn't thinking about us. I was thinking about talking to Eliza tomorrow. We need a road up to the staff building and we need to buy a couple of electric buggies.'

'For Tam? A couple? Or one for Nell too?'

I leaned into him as he pulled me closer. No, silly. I've been thinking about Zac's offer. But yes, one to get Tam up there for the next few months. And Nell. But as for a bigger picture, I think we could build a lookout up there, and then—' I paused as we reached our gate and looked across the island to the opposite hill where the lights glowed in the staff building on the opposite hill.

'And then?' my patient husband prompted me.

'And then, the road could go further, and we could build some exclusive huts up on the hill. Maybe two- and three-bedroom huts. We're starting to get groups of rock climbers and birdwatching groups book in, and we haven't had enough room to meet the demand.'

Rafe's arms went around me, and I rested my head on his shoulder as happiness seeped through me.

'Have I told you recently how happy I am that your Aunty Vi left her island to her great niece?'

I reached up and brushed my lips across his. 'Not this week, I don't think.'

'Well, I am, and I think she knew what an entrepreneur you would turn into. She always told me how special you were.' His lips rested against my forehead. 'Just so I'm prepared. How many extra huts are we talking about?'

The moon was bright, and I knew my eyes would be alight with laughter as I moved back and held his.

'Hmm, I think we have room to build another twenty or so. I'll see Eliza tomorrow and see what she thinks about talking to Zac.'

I turned to go through the gate, but Rafe's hand caught my arm. 'Phillipa?'

I turned as I picked up the concern in his voice.

'This isn't just to fill that gap in our life, is it?'

I shook my head. 'No, sweetheart, that gap will be filled when the time is right. This is Phillipa, the businesswoman thinking; not Phillipa who will one day be a mother too.' I turned to him as he moved closer, and I slipped my hand beneath my husband's shirt, my fingers playing along the silken skin of his back. 'Maybe we should go practise a little bit, what do you think?'

'Are we talking business or pleasure now?' His lips moved to mine and it was quite a while before I answered.

'Pleasure, definitely pleasure.'

Chapter Eleven
Aisling
Dublin. Ten years earlier.

Aisling had always known that one day her happiness would come to an end. Trying to juggle school, and meeting Niall at night and on weekends had the inevitable effect on her grades because she had little time to study. Her parents had been in London for three weeks involved in some important big case, so her freedom was much more than it would have been if they'd been home.

After the stoush when she was caught bunking off—that wonderful day when she'd met Niall—she'd promised faithfully she wouldn't do it again. Mother had forgiven her for being rude on the phone, but only because they were so preoccupied with their work, not from any motherly concern. Her next school report would be a catalyst for more trouble because she hadn't handed in most of the work that was due. As for the exams, she didn't even know if it was worth turning up for them.

She hadn't bunked off again, but she did get the bus straight into town every afternoon, and then back home late at night after spending time with Niall.

After the first few afternoons, when they'd either gone to a park or a coffee shop if it was raining, he'd looked at her with those sexy eyes.

'Would you think I was forward if I invited you back to my bedsit tomorrow afternoon?' His deep voice sent a shiver down her back, as did the thought of being alone with him. Niall had been a perfect gentleman, with a chaste goodnight kiss on her cheek each night when he put her on the bus. 'Not for any nefarious reason, of course, but just so we can spend time alone together.'

'Say that again,' she said.

'What?'

'Nefarious. I love the way your voice wraps around those syllables.' Aisling loved every word that came out of his mouth.

'Nefarious,' he said slowly with a smile. 'Perhaps I may not have been quite honest, as I do have some nefarious designs on you, but it is too soon yet.'

They were waiting at the bus stop and the heavy fog from the River Liffey shrouded them in its damp blanket.

Aisling reached up and pressed her mouth against Niall's. The taste of whiskey on his breath lingered on her lips when she moved away. 'I don't think it's too soon,' she whispered. 'And this weekend is perfect. My sister is going away on a uni field trip to London. I will be home alone.'

She straightened as the idea came to her. 'I have a better idea. Why don't you come to my place? The cook will have left all my meals for the weekend, and my father has a wonderfully stocked bar.'

'Would it be the right thing to do?'

'Yes, you are my friend and I'm inviting you to my house.'

##

Niall had agreed, and that weekend stayed in Aisling's memory long after everything went to shite. The weather cleared, and they were alone for two whole days and two nights before Niall took the bus back to the city on Sunday night. True to his word, he had not slept in her bed, even though Aisling had been willing.

'No, my sweet red rose. I don't want you to think this is about sex. I want to get to know you. I want to lie in the sun and read poetry to you. I want to get a true vision of you, so I can write a poem about you.'

They spent many hours on the sofa, her feet in his lap as he'd read his poetry to her. For the time it was enough for her, but she knew that one day soon there would be more.

As the bus taking him back to the city trundled down the rough cobblestones of the village street, she stood looking after it.

Next weekend.

Next weekend, she would go to Dublin, and in Niall's bedsit it would be time to take their relationship to the next level.

Aisling smiled all the way back to the house. As she turned the corner into their street, she drew in a breath as her father's green Jaguar approached the house from the other end of the narrow road.

Shite, what state had they left the house in?

Narrowing her eyes, she tried to think as she whipped out her phone and called Celia.

'Ceels, a favour. If anyone asks, you stayed at my house this weekend. Okay?'

'Did I?'

'Yes. Okay?'

'Okay, Ash. But can we catch up for a coffee after school one day this week? We haven't talked properly for ages.'

'Sure. And thanks, love, I owe you.'

'How's your tat? Did you get into trouble?'

'Nah, they've been away. I've been busy. Look I've got to go and clean up the house. They've just got home.'

'Okay. See you at school.'

Aisling hurried down the street and was through the front door before Da's Jag was in the garage. By the time the back door closed, and footsteps approached she'd whipped around the living room, and taken the dirty dishes and glasses into the kitchen. As she loaded the dishwasher, her father walked in.

'Hello, Da. I thought you and Mother were away for another week.'

His brows beetled over his narrowed eyes. 'We are. I had to come home for a file we left in the office. I'm very pleased to see you home and not out gallivanting around. I trust you've been studying?'

'Yes. Yes, I have.' Aisling nodded and crossed her fingers behind her back. 'All weekend.'

'Good, because I had a call from Sister Mary this week.'

She bit the inside of her cheek, before she could ask what the stupid old cow wanted. 'Yes?

'I was pleased to hear you've not missed a day of school, but Sister is concerned about how you've fallen behind in your work. She can't understand why.'

'The work's hard, Da. I've been working all weekend. I'm almost caught up.'

'Excellent. Your mother and I were talking, and we've had an offer from Charles Caul for you to begin an internship in his law firm before university starts. We think it's best if you don't come into the family law firm straight after your final school examinations. You're a very different person to Marlene, and shall we say, perhaps not as amenable. I think you would be more likely to take instruction from Charles and his son, rather than your mother and I.'

Aisling couldn't hold her temper back. 'Roger? Roger Caul? He's a bloody pervert. I've lost count of the number of times he's tried to grope me under the table at family dinners.'

'Aisling. Just stop it.' Her father's cheeks were red, and a vein pulsed in his temple. 'I am very tired of you twisting the truth, so you don't have to do things you don't want to do. You need to learn responsibility and learn to tell the truth. And stop taking money from my wallet. All you have to do is ask.'

'Yeah, and all you'd say would be no. Feckin' hell, Da. I know I'm not good enough for this family, but a bit of trust now and then would be nice.'

His eyes were hard. 'You have to earn that, Aisling.'

She closed her eyes, and thought of Niall's voice, and of the admiration he held for her. Niall saw the good in her, and he thought she was a fine person. She would not be going to university, and she would not be working with the bloody Cauls in their dark and depressing office. Her voice was cold when she opened her eyes and stared at her father. 'Yes, Da, you're right. I shall do my best to be responsible, and to earn your trust as you say.'

Aisling turned and walked up the stairs to her room. Five minutes later the back door closed, and the purr of her father's car faded as he drove out of town.

Chapter Twelve
Isla

Isla was preoccupied as she sat in the resort restaurant having dinner with Sienna. Staff were given a fifty percent discount on meals but were only able to eat in once the bookings were checked and there were spare tables. Some of the guests preferred to dine on the verandah of their huts. Angus and Cherry had also started an evening picnic deal where an exotic cold picnic was packed into a basket and delivered to a couple of grassy areas on the island. The guests pre-ordered and chose the location, and the meal was delivered by one of the waiters, along with a bottle of the finest champagne.

According to Sienna, it was a popular choice for proposals.

Island of love. It wouldn't be for her.

Isla sighed and stared out into the night as they waited for their main courses. Meeting that Irish guy this afternoon had rocked her a little bit. She knew that her family were trying to track her down;

she'd changed her email address a few times, and she had a dummy profile on Facebook and Instagram to get tabs on them.

Of course, her parents didn't do social media, but the occasional time she'd logged into her old account, there had been dozens of messages from Marlene.

Where are you?

We need to talk to you.

Call home.

Urgent. Please call.

Not a snowball's chance in hell.

As far as Isla was concerned, she had no family.

'Are you tired, Isla?' Sienna's soft voice broke into her musings. Gawd, if she let every Irish voice remind her of home and upset her, she had no chance of making a life for herself.

She plastered a smile on her face. 'I am, but a good night's sleep and a jog up to the wall in the morning will have me as right as rain.'

'You be careful up there. Apparently, there are wild goats.'

'They don't hurt you. I'm more worried about those huge birds that fly over the peak. Have you seen their wingspan? They're the size of a feckin' truck.'

Sienna giggled. 'I love listening to your accent, and your words. One day I will go to your Ireland.'

'Darlin', trust me. You don't want to. Grey skies, dense fog and sad faces. Stay in this gorgeous country. Or get Danny to take you to Italy. Now that is beautiful.'

'I've been to Italy. Eliza and I had a holiday there. It wasn't a very happy time.' Sienna's fair cheeks coloured. 'I think I will be staying here though. Danny has booked a picnic over at Back Bay on Saturday night. It's a full moon, and he told me he has something to ask me.' She reached over and grabbed Isla's hand. 'Do you think I am reading too much into it? Maybe it's just a simple picnic.'

Isla squeezed Sienna's fingers. 'Didn't you say this solicitor was about to sort out his ex?'

Sienna leaned back in her chair and smiled up at the new waiter as he held up the half bottle of wine they were sharing. 'Thank you, just a top up please.'

Isla put her hand over her glass. 'Not for me, thanks.'

When they were alone again, Sienna nodded. 'I think so.'

'No point worrying until things go pear-shaped, darlin'. Trust me, I'm an expert on that.'

And I should take my own advice, she thought.

The Irish guy was harmless. A bit of a nerd, and lacking self-confidence. She had to stop being suspicious.

It was still early by the time they finished their meals, and Sienna gestured to the bar where a group of off duty staff had gathered. 'I'm going to have a quick coffee. Do you want one too? You can have a sleep-in tomorrow before your run. Your first appointment's not until ten.'

Isla shook her head. 'My early one filled up after you left. An Irish guy, as shy as, with a bad back is coming in at eight-thirty so I'll be up at sparrow's fart.'

Sienna's eyes widened. 'What?'

'Don't worry, he just asked for the hot stone massage, even though I can do remedial, I know we don't offer that, so don't worry, I'm not doing the wrong thing.' Isla's words were clipped. It was the first time Sienna had challenged her.

Sienna waved her hand. 'Don't be silly. I said *what*, meaning what is that thing you talk about the sparrow?'

Isla giggled. 'Sorry, I was being precious. Just take my word for it. Sparrow's fart means very early in the day. I grew up with that expression, and I've heard it used Down Under too. Do you know what fart means?'

Sienna shook her head. 'No.'

'Okay, we'll leave it at that. Thanks for the great company, Sienna. I'll see you in the morning.'

Sienna reached over and hugged her goodnight. Isla knew she had made good friends here already. Life was on the up and up. She walked up the hill to her room, her self-confidence returning.

Chapter Thirteen
Aisling
Dublin. Ten years earlier.

'I don't care what you think, Niall. It's not too soon. I'm ready. I've never met anyone in my life I've cared about so much.' Aisling's voice shook as she sat in front of the small gas heater in Niall's tiny bedsit. 'I'm eighteen years old and I love you,' she added quietly. 'I know my mind.'

Warm hands took hers and when she didn't look up, he let go of one of her hands and tipped her chin up so she was looking into warm blue eyes.

'Did you really say that, Aisling? Or did I imagine it? Was it wishful thinking?'

'No. I said it. I love you, Niall.' Her head shook from side to side. 'I can't imagine being without you.'

Six weeks had passed since that afternoon when Aisling and Celia had walked into that old pub and Aisling had fallen head over heels in love. In those six weeks, Niall had treated her with respect, even on the nights she had stayed over in his bedsit, and the weekend he had come to Castleknock to stay in her family home—when her parents were away of course.

Six weeks of reading together, listening to poetry and falling in love with the English language. Her insightful comments at school, in the weeks after she had met Niall and spent all those afternoons and nights talking poetry and literature had not only awakened new knowledge in her but had surprised the dour Sister Mary.

Her English marks had gone off the scale for the final examinations, but that was not enough to make up for her dismal performance in all the other subjects.

'I don't care,' she protested vehemently when Sister Mary called her to the office one day. 'I don't want to be a lawyer, and I don't want to go to university. I just want—'

'What do you want, child?' The concern in the nun's voice had surprised Aisling. Six years in the school and she'd never once seen a glimmer of interest in the woman's face, but now that Niall had introduced her to the beauty of literature, a connection had been forged with the elderly nun.

'I am going to have to speak to your father. If you fail your examinations—and I am sure that that will happen, he will not be impressed that I haven't warned him.'

'I don't care. He is trying to live his life through me. I don't want to go to university, I just want—'

'What do you want, Aisling?'

I want Niall.

But of course, she wouldn't say that to the nun.

Now Niall's hands cupped her cheeks, and his voice was intense.

'Love is too young to know what conscience is. Yet who knows not conscience is born of love?'

Aisling stamped her foot. 'Stop it. Just stop it. I know what I want, Niall. I am not too young. I want you.' Her shaking hands went to her school shirt, and she began to unbutton the heavy cotton. When it was open, she slid down the zip of her serge skirt and as it fell to the threadbare carpet, she kicked it aside.

Niall's groan as he reached for her told her all she wanted to hear.

To hear, to feel, to experience.

Aisling's lip tipped up in a satisfied smile as Niall's lips trailed a warm path down her neck.

##

Later that night, Niall walked her to the bus stop. It was a Friday night, and her parents would be home from the city after they had been to dinner.

She knew she should be on top of the world and all she wanted to do was stay in Niall's bed. Sometimes Aisling wondered what right her parents had to direct her life, when she was very much on the periphery of all that mattered to them. If she disappeared, would they even notice? Or care?

'What's wrong? You seem unhappy tonight,' he said. 'You should be happy.'

'Oh Niall, I am. I don't want to leave you tonight. I worry about what's going to happen. My father is so bloody minded, he's likely to do anything. Promise me that if anything happens you'll come and find me?'

'Nothing's going to happen, sweetheart. The worst that can happen is that he'll throw you out and you know you have a place with me.' He pulled her close and his lips were hard against hers. 'I love you, Aisling, and I will not let you go. Trust me.'

A group of young boys walking past the bus stop catcalled them. 'Get a room, boyo,' one of them called out.

That afternoon was the last time she ever saw Niall. Her father was waiting for her when she walked in at nine o'clock. In the months to come, Aisling knew that if she'd known what was going to happen, she would never have left Niall that night.

Her life would have been different.

It would have been happy.

She would not have had to run away.

##

'You are leaving school. And you will have a live-in tutor. You are grounded until you resit your examinations and pass them.'

Aisling twisted out of her father's cruel grasp and looked to her mother for support, but there was nothing in her expression that gave her hope. 'No. That will not happen.'

'Oh, yes it will. You are not leaving this house. Jennifer, go and ask Sean to come in please.'

When Mam left the study her father's eyes glittered with dark malevolence and Aisling swore that she would leave the house tonight and go to Niall.

'And before you even consider running away, you will be confined to your room. Sean, your tutor, will teach you at your desk, and Cook will deliver your meals to your room. I will take you myself for a daily exercise in the fresh air. You will do as we expect, Aisling. I am over your rebellion. I will teach you what it expected of an O'Sullivan.'

'No!' she screamed like a banshee. 'Disown me. Throw me out. I will not do it.'

'You will.' Her father turned as the door opened and her mother walked in with a stranger.

'Aisling, this is Sean Roberts. He will be your tutor and will prepare you for your examinations.'

Suddenly, Aisling realised that rebellion was not the way to achieve what she wanted; complacence would earn trust, and trust would mean escape.

She lifted her eyes to meet those of her tutor and revulsion ran through her as his eyes settled on her breasts.

'It's a pleasure to be your tutor, Aisling. I'm sure we can bring your mathematics up to the required standard.

Aisling stared at him and waved a hand. 'Whatever.'

Her father nodded and her mother looked away.

Chapter Fourteen
Isla

At six-thirty the following morning Isla reached the top of the track where the path to the mountain and Red Wave Wall crossed the beach track. She bent double and caught her breath; the jog up the mountain was challenging but her fitness was improving each morning. It was a grand start to the day and put her in a good frame of mind.

She drew in a deep breath and her fingertips tingled with excitement as she turned to survey the vista below. Her new home, and by the way she was feeling, it was a new start. A chance to heal, and finally an opportunity to put the past behind her. Maybe she could come to terms with her life and become Aisling again. Be honest about her past and stop hiding behind an imaginary family where happiness was the norm.

Maybe soon.

Maybe then, she'd sit down with Sienna and tell her the truth about her family. Forget the imaginary brothers and sweet Ma and Da, and the tribe of nephews and nieces. Maybe telling someone the truth for the first time would take the pain of loss away. Maybe telling about her cold and cruel family would help her heal.

Isla sat on a rock already warm from the early sun. Even if she got over what had happened, she would never forget the day she had found Niall five years ago. It had been too late, way too late and she knew that well. The reach of bloody social media. She would have been better off not looking, of not knowing. It had sealed a lid on the coffin of her happy future.

Too late for her, and too late to do anything about it. With a sigh, Isla tried to put those thoughts away; she could not live the rest of her life like this. Skipping from place to place, never putting roots down. Never forming relationships. Witnessing the happiness on the island, she knew it was time to settle down. She'd heard a little about the history of each of the women here, and she knew she had to try to move on from her past too. They had overcome difficulties, and they had forged new lives for themselves. She let her gaze linger on the beauty in front of her.

It was too early for much water traffic out on the Whitsunday Passage, but in the distance two catamarans headed south, their sails white and billowing in the wind.

She put her hands on her hips and her breathing returned to normal. She had been in Australia long enough to think about emigrating, and this morning she promised herself that she would explore that path.

Whatever had to be done, she would do it.

Maybe she should also make contact with her family and let them know she was all right.

No. With a frown, Aisling shook her head. No, of course she wouldn't. She had no family. They had ensured she wanted nothing to do with them.

The future would have to happen without contact; she could not forget or forgive. Her parents had talked about responsibility when she was eighteen, but it was their lack of responsibility, and a lack of parental love that had ruined her life.

Sure she had been responsible for some of her choices, but each of those had been in direct response to how she had been treated.

She could not forgive. Closing her eyes, she made herself think about the time when her chance of a life with Niall had come to an end.

It had probably been a dream, but she'd never know now.

Chapter Fifteen
Aisling
Dublin. Ten years earlier.

Six weeks after Aisling had last seen Niall, she woke up one morning and grimaced as she rolled over. Her breasts hurt when she lay on her stomach.

With a frown she rolled over again and ran her fingers over the tender skin, and it still hurt.

Her mouth dried as she realised that her period was overdue.

Oh shit.

Could she be pregnant, or was it simply her hormones responding to the bizarre and stressful situation her bloody father had created with the damn tutor. He wanted her to go into law. If—when—she got out of this stupid predicament, she'd sue him for everything she could.

Aisling touched her stomach in wonder, and looked down, but then worry wrapped its insidious fingers around her.

Yes, she most certainly could be pregnant. Niall didn't believe in contraception and because she was so smitten with him, she had listened.

What was he thinking? Did he wonder why she hadn't been back to see him? Did he wonder why she hadn't called? Why hadn't he come looking for her? He knew where she lived.

Had he called her? Da had taken her phone from her and as he had threatened he would and she had been a prisoner in her room.

Doubt began to creep in. Had she fallen for Niall too quickly? He had been the first person to show her any love, and he'd made her believe in herself. That the person she was, was a good person and could be loved. With him, she didn't need the stuff that made her look different and rebellious.

Of course, he loved her: they had connected on an intellectual level and a spiritual level.

Don't forget the sexual level, a nagging voice reminded her. What if that was all it had been?

Had she been naïve?

No, she wouldn't doubt him.

She would trust.

The only person she'd seen since her parents had gone back to the city last Monday had been the slimy Sean as he had tried to teach her, and she'd hated every minute that she had to spend in his company. His constant brushing against her, and the way he looked at her breasts rather than her face made her feel ill.

Sean had taken to lying on her bed as she had completed the tasks that he gave her each morning—there was no explicit teaching taking place—and she was very wary of him and kept her distance. The smell of his deodorant lingered each afternoon when he left.

'Use the chair,' she finally snapped that morning as she worked her way through a mathematics exercise he'd put on her desk. Her temper had been much shorter than usual as she worried about the non-arrival of her period and her tender breasts.

'Make me,' he said with a leer.

Rolling her eyes Aisling turned back to the stupid maths exercise. At least the work filled the days even though she had to put up with Sean being in her room with her. Aisling had tried everything to escape her imprisonment. One day when Sean had been using *her* bathroom, she had moved silently to the door and tried to open it. As she expected it was locked, as were her windows. The next morning, she took notice as he came in and watched as he'd locked the door and put the key in his trouser pocket.

Last weekend after three weeks of being locked in her room, she had begged Da for a reprieve when they had come home for the weekend.

His eyes had been cold as they had walked around the back garden for her exercise. 'When you sit your examinations, we shall see.'

Aisling had been tempted to retort that her civil liberties were being breached but had realised just in time that she would not be doing herself any favours.

She had put her head down meekly and said, 'Yes, Da,' as she vowed to herself that she would find a way out.

Today fear almost pushed her over the edge. She knew she had to get out, she had to find Niall.

Her life was turning into a Thomas Hardy novel, and Aisling knew she had to take control. Niall had been a huge fan of Hardy's work and they had had several vigorous conversations in his bedsit about Hardy's portrayal of women. It was the only time they had disagreed.

'Due to their humanity, suffering is inevitable, and guilt is a common compassion of his heroines,' Niall had said.

'No.' Aisling closed her eyes as she remembered how she had sat cross-legged on his bed and Niall had laughed and put his arms around her. 'He presents women as sensual creatures, but he portrays us as weak. No woman would have put up with the circumstances that he portrayed,' she had argued. 'Hardy portrays women affected by the pressure exerted on them by their environment and heredity.'

'I disagree,' Niall said to her surprise. 'Your sensuality and your weakness are what appeals.'

'What!' Aisling's mouth dropped open as she stared at him, unable to believe what he was saying. 'Are you talking about me or is that a stereotypical comment?' She had sat up straight on the old sofa and shaken her head. 'I can't believe you said that.'

All she got in return was a shrug and his gentle smile. So, she still hadn't known if he really meant was he said.

As she thought about that night, her chest ached. Despite their disagreement over Hardy's themes, it had also been the night she had first shared Niall's bed, and the night she had felt loved for the first time in her eighteen years. Aisling's vision blurred as tears ran down her face.

She was in the same weak position they had discussed. Pregnant, isolated from the man she loved, and imprisoned in her room. Her father couldn't keep her here forever. She wondered what he would do if she told him she was pregnant.

Tomorrow, she would somehow get the door key from Sean. No matter what she had to do. No matter what it took.

Oh Niall, please come and find me. Don't think I have left you.

Chapter Sixteen
Pippa

'Slow down, love.' Rafe reached out and grabbed me as I hurried through the kitchen, a piece of toast in one hand and a coffee in the other. The last few mornings I had woken up starving and had eaten a full breakfast but today I had too much to do.

'I can't.' My mouth was full as I replied. 'I have to meet Zac and Eliza in the office for a meeting in five minutes, and then after that, I have to talk to Cherry about the setup for the wedding on Saturday week, and then I have to go over to the day spa because there is a problem with—'

His lips swooped on mine, and I couldn't finish telling about the problem in *Hebe*. I grinned as he pulled straight back and wiped the back of his hand across his mouth. He took my coffee and swallowed a huge gulp.

'Oh yuk. Vegemite.'

'Hey, that's my coffee. And serves you right for kissing me when I'm in a hurry.'

'Phillipa.' My husband's voice was calm as he put his arms around me. 'Slow down.'

'I can't. I have a huge day.'

'I'll go and sort out the problem in the day spa for you.'

'You can't. You have to get your book in by the end of the week.'

'Sweetheart, an hour checking out a problem, and sorting it out is not going to impact on my deadline. It's the least I can do after you read those chapters for me all week. That put you behind in your work.'

I went to kiss him, and he moved away.

'Go and brush your teeth and then I'll kiss you after you do.'

Indignantly, I put my hands on my hips but I grinned up at him. Rafe hadn't shaved yet and his fair skin with the night stubble shadowing his jaw line and the black David Bowie T-shirt would have had me dragging him back to bed if I didn't have an appointment.

'Thank you, my love. But I have to go because Zac has to be at the pool at nine.'

He put his hands up in surrender and kissed my neck instead of my Vegemite-flavoured lips. 'Okay, go. I'll see you later.'

'Love you. And thank you, don't forget to go to *Hebe*. I know what you're like when your computer boots up.'

'I'll go now.' His grin was slow and sexy as he took my coffee from me again. 'As soon as I finish *your* coffee. You can get one in the restaurant.'

As I moved away my tummy let out a huge gurgle. 'I'll get breakfast down there too. I'm starving.'

Rafe narrowed his eyes, and we exchanged a significant look. 'That's not like you. You usually can't face breakfast.'

'It's not, is it?' My spirits sang and hope filled me as I hurried down to the restaurant to discuss the next stage of development of Ma Carmichael's resort.

It was not like me at all.

***

Isla

Isla was as nervous as a cat on a hot tin roof. She'd had a quick shower after her run, trying to tell herself that she'd be sure to have more Irish clients while she worked here, and there was nothing to stress about. There was no way Ronan Doyle would know her family or why she was hiding in Australia. Ireland was a big place.

Australia was an even bigger place.

Deep breath in, she told herself.

She'd arrived at *Hebe* before Sienna and then Rafe had turned up to look at the steriliser unit. She'd fumbled and dropped things as he'd checked the power and the cable and felt totally useless when he'd glanced across at her.

'Sorry,' she apologised. 'I'm still a bit shaky from my run. It'll be gone by my eight-thirty appointment.'

Rafe had chuckled. The problem with the steriliser was fixed and she got the room ready and set the stones to heat. Sienna was already in her room with her first client.

The appointment with the Irish guy had started well and it didn't take Isla long to relax into her usual routine. He was quieter than any client she'd ever had, no questions, no conversation, and no incessant I-have-to-fill-the-silence with words. As soon as he was settled face down on the table, the lower half of his torso covered with a towel, she placed the hot granite stones on his lower back and then asked him to reach around and touch where his back was sore.

As soon as she touched his lower back where he'd indicated, she could feel where the twisted muscle was.

'I'll do the hot stone massage to start with, and then if you're happy I can do some remedial massage as part of the package.'

He nodded, and she got to work.

***

Ronan

Ronan tapped on the door of the day spa hut and waited for the door to open.

'Come in.' The Irish-accented voice was brisk as she stepped back to let him enter the dimly lit treatment room. A strong smell of massage oil wafted over to him as she pointed to the privacy screen.

'Strip down to your jocks and lie face down on the table. Give me a call when you're all settled, and we'll get your back sorted.'

She stepped outside as he walked over to the screen and stripped down, folding his shorts and T-shirt and placing them neatly on the chair provided. He was way out of his comfort zone. He'd never had a massage like this before; the last massage he could remember was a rub with liniment after a rugby game when he was at college.

'Research, man,' he muttered to himself. He wasn't looking forward to this, but hopefully he'd pick up some information.

'I'm ready,' he called quietly as he settled face down on the table and put his face into the soft vinyl ring and looked down at the floor. A click was followed by the sound of birds calling and water running.

'Rightio. We'll get started and have you as good as gold at the end of the hour.' He closed his eyes as two smooth warm hands gripped his calves and pulled his legs straight. Embarrassment warmed his face.

'Ah.' Her voice was soft.

Ronan tried to lift his head and look around, wondering what she was exclaiming about, but his face down position on the massage table made it impossible to see. He grimaced as she stretched his left leg back and then his right.

'Yes, you have a twisted muscle in your lower right quadrant. Not a drama.'

Ronan closed his eyes and let his mind drift as she placed hot stones on his lower back. He tried to focus on the remedial aspect of the massage, and then he tried to think about his certainty that she was the woman he was searching for, but her firm hands sliding up and down the backs of his calves and thighs, and the smooth sensation of the massage oil on his skin sent tingles up to his groin. He swallowed and focused on the smooth polished floorboards beneath the table. *Think about why you're here, boyo.*

Bloody inappropriate his reaction was. The tightness building in his groin began to lessen, until her warm hands reached his lower back.

Embarrassment flooded through him at the thought of her turning him over when she finished with the hot stones. He shouldn't have done it this way; the privacy issue was off the scale. But then all thoughts fled the window as her firm fingers hit a nerve at the base of his back and she pressed.

Hard. Freakin' hard.

Shite that hurt. He grunted in pain.

'Can you take that again?'

'Okay.' The two syllables were almost a squeak.

By the time, her fingers had worked their way from the base of his back to his shoulders, Ronan was in great discomfort. Did she know why he was here and it was payback time?

'This might hurt a little,' the melodious voice warned him.

Bloody hell! The points of her elbows were walking down his back now.

What would she do next? Bloody walk on him? But strangely the more pressure she applied and the greater the pain, the better he began to feel.

'Okay.' She lifted the stones from his lower back and a sensation of wellbeing swept over him. He was finding it hard to keep his eyes open, let alone keep his thoughts in order. 'Roll over for me, please.'

Ronan obliged and she adjusted the towel to cover him. He settled his head on the low pillow she eased beneath his neck, unable to figure out what she'd done and why he was suddenly feeling so good. Hell, he was so relaxed he would have told her anything she asked, so he jammed his lips together.

He closed his eyes again as she started on his feet and worked her way up his legs, kneading muscles.

'I'm not hurting your lower back?'

He shook his head, and kept his eyes closed.

Her hands left him for a moment, and he let his mind drift.

Gradually his doze lifted as relaxation took over his entire body.

He opened his eyes just in time to see her lift her hands and lightly rest one finger on his knees, his lower stomach, his chest, and his throat before lightly touching the top of his head.

'Just relax for a while. We have ten minutes left so enjoy the peace and when you're ready to get up, there is a glass of iced water for you beside the chair.'

He watched as she walked to the door, but she didn't turn before the door clicked slowly shut behind her. Well, he'd worked out one thing this morning; Isla O'Sullivan was freakin' good at what she did. He'd never felt so relaxed in his life.

Ronan shook his head as he pushed himself up from the massage bed. He couldn't afford to feel like this and lower his guard. He had a job to do; he had to prove that this woman was the one whose sister was desperate to contact her back in Dublin.

And he'd wasted the hour. He hadn't learned one damn thing about it.

As he slipped his shorts back on, and bent over without his back catching, he realised that the appointment had been worthwhile in that aspect.

He wasn't in pain anymore.

Ronan drank the iced water and stood in front of the mirror and smoothed his hand over his ruffled hair.

Okay he was going to have to get out of his comfort zone. Time was running out.

He stood straight and headed for the door, digging for courage.

Chapter Seventeen
Isla

As Isla waited for the Irish guy to come out of the treatment room, she checked the appointments book and ran her finger down the bookings for the day. Thanks goodness it was mostly facials; she'd gone in hard with the massage and her fingers were tired from the extra pressure she'd used. But she knew that she'd been successful; he'd relaxed as she'd worked.

The door opened. Ronan came out of the treatment room and pulled his wallet out of his pocket.

Isla shook her head and held her hand up. 'No need. The treatment is added to your resort bill. You just have to sign for it here.'

He put his wallet away, and his smile was slow. Ronan Doyle seemed like a nice guy, but she felt sorry for him; he seemed very quiet.

'You seem to be moving a lot more easily. Is your back less tight?' she asked as she pushed the slip over for him to sign.

He lifted his head and stared at her, and she held his gaze. He was a fine-looking guy. She hadn't looked past the shy demeanour before. Now his dark brown eyes glowed with warmth and laughter crinkles appeared around his eyes.

'You have magic hands.'

This time, she was the one whose cheeks coloured. 'Thank you. As long as you feel better. It probably wouldn't hurt to come back in another couple of days. Until then, keep your back warm.'

He chuckled. 'Warm? I don't think I'll ever be cool again. It's very different to home.'

He looked down again, obviously embarrassed that he was talking too much. Isla felt sorry for him.

'Where is home?'

'A little town in the south-west of Ireland. I doubt if you've even heard of it.' He looked up again. 'Almost as far from Dublin as you can get.'

'Dublin?' She drew herself up. 'What makes you think I'm from Dublin?'

'Your accent. I have an ear for accents, and yours is posh Dublin.'

Isla couldn't help smiling. 'Posh Dublin, you say?'

He nodded and smiled back at her. 'It is. Am I right?'

She put one finger to her lips and shook her head. 'Maybe, maybe not. It's been a long time since I lived in Ireland. My posh as you say is probably a combination of the places I've been and worked over the past ten years. The world has been a bit of a melting pot for me.'

He stood there for a moment, and looked down, and then up again meeting her eyes, and then dropped his head again before he finally spoke. 'Ah, look I'm way out of practice at this and it might be inappropriate, or you may not even want to, but I was wondering, if ah, maybe if you'd like to have a drink with me tonight.' He took a deep breath and kept talking, this time, lifting his head and holding her gaze. 'Or another night. There's no rush. I'm having a long holiday here. Or look, you might even have a partner or be married, I'm sorry, forget I asked.'

Isla looked back at him, trying to figure him out. Was he really that shy or was it the pickup spiel that he used to get a woman to feel sorry for him?

Because she did. He seemed so out of his comfort zone, he had to be for real.

'Sure, I'll have a drink with you in the bar. You can tell me all about the village you say I won't have heard of.'

His eyes widened and his cheeks flushed. 'Oh, that is excellent. Not the village, I mean, but that you will have a drink with me. I won't push it and say dinner would be good, but we both have to eat, don't we?'

Isla couldn't help smiling. 'We do. But let's play it by ear. I have no idea what time I'll finish today. So, we'll make plans for a drink and see what happens from there.'

Having a normal conversation with a guy felt good. Letting her guard down felt good. Tonight she would be a normal almost thirty-year-old having a drink with an interesting man.

Because even though he was shy, she did find him interesting. She didn't have to talk about herself, she'd get Ronan talking about himself.

Tonight would be her first step to getting back to a normal life. A life where she would be honest, and a life where she'd feel comfortable without putting on all that false exuberance.

His smile was as wide as hers as he signed the docket and passed it back to her. 'Thank you. You've made my day.' He stumbled over his words again. 'Not with the fixing my back, I mean. Although that was really good too. But by agreeing to meet me for a drink. My holiday is looking up. Oh, please don't feel as—'

'Ronan? Stop stressing and stop talking. You can talk to me all you want tonight, but for now, get going. Go out and have a great day and keep that back warm. I'll see you tonight. Okay?'

'Okay.' He nodded vigorously and turned so quickly, she thought he was going to fall over on the way to the door.

Shaking her head, Isla went back into the treatment room to tidy up, ready for the next client. Warmth settled in her chest, and she felt good. It was a step in the right direction.

What could go wrong on an island far removed from her old life by both time and distance?

Chapter Eighteen

Aisling - Dublin. Ten years earlier.

The day of reckoning came sooner than Aisling had hoped for. There had been no sign of Niall unless he'd come for her and been turned away without her knowing.

Sean had tried to become more familiar with her as the days passed and he was really starting to annoy her. Sometimes, a tingle of fear would thrum through her, but she was too preoccupied with her situation to let it take hold.

She had more things to worry about than a tutor who liked to perve on her. Every time she stood to stretch, Sean would be up in a flash, and press himself close behind her, his breath hot on her neck while he asked after her wellbeing. She'd soon learned to move away, and not say anything. On the few early occasions she'd told him to piss off, his fingers would tug at her hair until he'd turned her head to meet his eyes.

She didn't like what she saw in them.

He was a cruel and nasty man, but no one seemed to care. He'd been put with her so that she would pass her exams.

Occasionally Mrs Smithers, the cook, would throw her a sympathetic glance when she brought a hot lunch up for them each day.

Aisling's emotional strength declined as the days passed, and she tried to tell herself this situation could not last forever. She made sure that she ate properly; she had to look after her health and keep her energy up for when she finally escaped this hell, found Niall and made a life with him.

The week before the end of year examinations, her father arrived home unexpectedly one afternoon. Relief flooded through Aisling when he appeared in the doorway and gestured for Sean to come downstairs with him.

The Aisling of old would have had a rude comment to make to her father about how ignorant he was, but her courage had diminished; he had killed her spark and she no longer had the will to be objectionable.

Niall had been right when she had argued against his view that no woman would have put up with the circumstances that Hardy portrayed in his novels.

Aisling lay on her bed wondering what was being discussed downstairs. She knew she should have ranted and raved and told her father to release her immediately.

Maybe Sean would tell him how well she had worked and how compliant she'd been, and she would be freed from her room, the room that had become a prison.

Looking down, Aisling spread her fingers over her flat stomach. Was that all in her imagination?

Had she ever met Niall, or had he been a dream? This was doing her head in.

The door opened and Sean walked back in and locked the door. Aisling stood, disappointed that her father hadn't come back up to say it was over. As much as she hated him, he was the only one who would say she could go. There had been no sign of her mother for the whole six weeks she'd been in this stupid situation.

'Does Da want me to go downstairs now?' She looked at the key in Sean's hand.

Sean ignored her question and followed her gaze down to the key and he'd held it up. 'You'd really like to have this, wouldn't you?'

Aisling nodded. 'I would.'

'Maybe we can come to an arrangement?' He reached over and pressed his thumb against her lips. 'But it will have to be our secret.'

Aisling nodded as hope trickled in. 'I can keep a secret. I won't tell anyone you gave it to me.'

He shook his head. 'That's not what I meant.'

She frowned and tried to move back away from him but came up hard against the desk. He followed her and dangled the key in front of her nose as he pressed against her. 'That's not what I meant. You have to keep quiet about our arrangement.'

'What arrangement? We don't have one.' Fear iced her veins as he pressed harder against her.

'Do you want the key?'

'You know I do.'

'Then my dear, it's simple. We have an arrangement.'

Sean took her hand and unclenched the fingers that Aisling hadn't realised were fisted against his chest. He put the key in her hand and closed her fingers around it. 'I've kept my end of the deal, now it's all up to you, Aisling. You're not going to tell anyone about this, are you?'

Her eyes widened in horror as he began to remove the belt from his trousers.

Chapter Nineteen
Pippa

The morning of Nell and Nat's wedding, Rafe stood beside me in our ensuite and held my hand as we both stared at the white pregnancy test stick lying flat on the bench beside the basin.

'How long has it been now?' My voice shook as he looked at his phone.

'Two minutes and thirty seconds.'

'Thirty seconds to go,' I said.

He rested his forehead against mine and I could feel his tension. 'The longest thirty seconds of our lives, do you think?'

'Maybe, but as soon as they are over, I have to go down to the restaurant and make sure Tamsin doesn't overdo it. She wants the catering to be perfect this afternoon, and I know she'll be down there already.'

Rafe held his phone up. 'Time's up, sweetheart.'

I closed my eyes. 'Are you going to look, or am I?'

'How about we look together?' He was as shaky as I was.

'Okay.' I reached out and picked up the stick and held it up so we could both read it together.

When I saw the result on the little screen, I looked up at Rafe with tears in my eyes.

He was smiling too, but his tears matched mine.

'We did it, my darling Pip. We're having a baby.'

***

I walked on air down the steps to the resort, Rafe holding my hand tightly. Every couple of steps we would look at each other and grin. When we reached the bottom step, he took me into his arms and kissed me soundly before he headed to the pool to supervise the lights that were going up today, and I headed to the restaurant to check on Tamsin.

'Are we going to keep it a secret, or do you want to tell the girls?' he said against my mouth as I looped my arms around his neck.

'What do you think?' I was beside myself with excitement, but strangely, I wasn't focused on the fear of miscarrying, even though I had lost our first child.

'I'll leave it up to you, Pip. One look at your face today and anyone will guess you are excited.'

'And yours too,' I said kissing him back.

'Yes, and mine too,' he admitted. 'When will you be back at the house?'

'Once I check on Tam, I'll chase Nell up. We're due over at the day spa for Sienna to do our hair and makeup. I'll get dressed up at the house, so I'll see you late morning.'

His lips found mine again. 'You be careful, Mrs Rendell.'

'I will. And Rafe?' I tipped my head to the side and smiled at him. 'We could have a problem.'

'Yes? What's wrong?'

'Have you checked your clothes are ready for the ceremony? Last time I noticed your dress shirt was in the laundry basket.'

'Oh shit, I'd better get that sorted.'

'You'd better. Can't have the MC looking like a derro.'

'Why do I keep getting these microphone jobs?' He pulled a face. 'And what's a derro?'

'Because you have such a gorgeous sexy voice, my dear. And a derro is what you'll look like if you don't iron your shirt for the wedding.'

'Never fear, my dear. I won't let you down.'

He kissed me again and I reluctantly stepped away. 'I have to go. I love you.'

'Love you too, sweetheart.'

He let go of my hands and I hurried through the glade towards the restaurant. I was bursting with the news that I was pregnant, but I didn't want to take the shine off Nell's wedding day.

Chapter Twenty
Isla

Isla called into *Hebe* briefly before she headed over to the restaurant to help set up for the lunch. Sienna was doing the makeup for the bride and her two attendants, Pippa and Tamsin, for the noon wedding, which was to be followed by a casual luncheon.

Being with brides and bridesmaids and getting caught up in that sort of celebration was the last place she wanted to be. Sienna was doing Nell's hair, and Pippa and Tamsin were sitting with towels wrapped turban-like around their heads.

'All good here, Sienna? Or do you need an extra pair of hands?' Isla crossed her fingers behind her back.

'We're fine, you go and take some time for you. You've been working hard.'

'Okay. Have a great day, ladies,' she said with a cheery smile. The three of them had huge smiles on their faces, and a niggle of envy gripped Isla briefly.

Last night, when she had swung by the restaurant to collect a takeaway curry, as she'd rung up her meal, Cherry had asked Sienna if she could help set the tables in the restaurant mid-morning.

'I wouldn't ask but Tess is off for the weekend, and my usual kitchen hand is filling in at the reception.'

'Of course,' she agreed happily. The drink with Ronan could wait. 'I'm not needed in the day spa, and I've got the whole afternoon off. We closed *Hebe* to guests today, because of the wedding.'

'That's why Nell decided to have her wedding in the middle of the day,' Cherry said. 'She wanted to be married on the island, but she didn't want it to disrupt the guests.'

Isla smiled. 'They won't be disrupted. A wedding on the island of love!'

Cherry chuckled. 'Pentecost Island sure is getting that reputation. Watch out, or you'll find you lose your heart here too. The rest of us have.'

'No fear of that. My heart is iron clad.' Isla put a hand on her chest and fluttered her lashes to soften her words.

'We'll see. We all fall eventually, even if there can be difficulties. Angus and I wasted a whole year due to misunderstandings.'

Isla nodded. She didn't want to know the details. 'So, what's the plan for lunch?'

'The reception is in *Violet's* restaurant. Lunch will be served from the pool bar for the guests, and then the restaurant will be open for dinner as usual tonight. Once the meal and speeches are over the wedding guests are going up to Pippa and Rafe's house to continue the celebration. It's a very small wedding so there's not many tables to set up.'

'Do you need a hand in the restaurant at night?' Isla offered.

'Thanks anyway, but we're all good. Take some time for yourself. I've seen how busy you and Sienna have been. You've been putting in some long days.'

'I will. After the ceremony, I'm going to head up to the rock-climbing wall to have a look.' Nell had invited all the staff to witness the ceremony if they wanted to, but the wedding reception was for close friends and family.

The resort had to keep functioning, despite one of the partners getting married. The huts were at full capacity—some with Nat and Nell's families—but the rest were fully booked by holidaymakers.

'You're into climbing rocks?'

Isla shook her head and grinned. 'Gosh, no. I hate heights. But so many of my clients have been talking about the view from up there this week, I thought I'd go up and take a look.'

'It's pretty spectacular. You can see Indian Head from up there. The rock climbers have started climbing that rock too. Angus wanted me to do it with him, but I said no way! When I have time off, I want to spend it lying around the pool.'

'I'll check it out,' Isla said. 'I'm getting to love this island.'

As she left, her Irish client gave her a half-smile from the table near the counter. She walked over and his cheeks coloured.

'I'll have to take a rain check on our drink. I've been rostered on some extra duties.'

'Oaky, Thanks for letting me know.' Isla had worried about hurting his feelings as she'd walked back to her room.

After the tables were set, and Isla had watched Nat and Nell make their wedding vows, she went back to her room to get changed to go for a walk up to Red Wave Wall.

The ceremony had been short and sweet, but it had left her feeling unsettled. The island seemed to be full of love and romance—the bridal couple and the other girls with partners set off a small niggle of envy in Isla's chest.

She shook her head and stamped down on that thought.

Just think back, girl, and look where it got you. She had vowed to stay alone for her whole life.

She had been hurt too badly by people she should have been able to trust, and like she had told Cherry her heart was iron clad.

So being unsettled emotionally watching the happiness of those around her was stupid. It did not—and would not—tempt her at all.

Pulling on her walking boots, Isla focused on the walk ahead. She picked up a small backpack and grabbed a couple of bottles of water out of the communal fridge in the staff lodge. The staff here were looked after so well; it was the best working conditions she'd ever had. Adding a couple of muesli bars and an apple to her bag, she slipped it onto her back, looking forward to an afternoon by herself exploring this wonderful island.

As she stepped purposefully out of the lodge which was halfway up the hill towards the walking track, music and laughter drifted up from below.

She ignored it and strode up the track. Soon the only sound was the rustling of the leaves in the hoop pine forests, and the occasional call of a bird.

Peace began to seep through her skin as she stared out over the glorious blue vista that spread out below her the higher she climbed. The sounds, the smell of the sea, and the feel of the warm air caressing her skin surrounded her with serenity.

She had climbed so high now that the resort was only the occasional glimpse of buildings peeking through the rainforest canopy below.

She was almost on top of the world, and she was up here by herself. Isla enjoyed her own company; she didn't need to be with anyone to appreciate the beauty of nature surrounding her.

She didn't need to talk incessantly to a companion, or to seek their opinions or their agreement on anything. Her life was good the way it was, and she was happy being that way.

In those dark months in Dublin after she'd left the hospital, retreating into her own company and her own thoughts had been her salvation.

That was the last time she'd ever seen her father. Her mother had been absent since Sean Roberts had first turned up at the house.

Isla had made no contact with them and had cut herself off from her family.

'And I'm happy,' she thought as she reached the place where the path split. One way led to the mountain path which led to Red Wave Wall. Unscrewing the top of her bottle, Isla took a good drink of water before she began to climb the path. Half an hour later she was perspiring freely and reached up to wipe her forehead with her forearm. The sun was high in the February sky, and high thunderclouds sat above the horizon to the east as they did each afternoon, but so far had not delivered any rain.

She drew in a deep breath and her fingertips tingled with excitement as Isla turned to survey the vista in front of her.

In the distance, a fleet of sailing boats headed south, their headsails white and billowing in the wind.

The sky and the sea melded together in a deep turquoise, and she drew in a deep sigh of contentment. Isla was pretty sure she'd found the place she was going to stay.

With a determined step she followed the path that led to the climbing wall.

Chapter Twenty-One
Ronan

Ronan leaned back against the hot rock of the steep wall. The patch of shade he was sitting in had lessened as the sun had sunk lower in the afternoon sky. He'd drunk all of his water and his handkerchief was soaked from where he'd been mopping the sweat from his head and neck since he'd started the climb two hours ago. If he stayed up here much longer, he knew he'd end up dehydrated. There was a large spreading tree a little bit further up the track, but he didn't have the energy to keep going. He'd sit here for a while longer and then go up to the tree. It looked like his quarry wasn't coming up the mountain after all.

He looked down at his watch; he'd move to the shady tree and give her another fifteen minutes and then he'd head back down. He was sure that he'd heard the conversation correctly in the restaurant last night. Isla had told Cherry she was going to climb up to the climbing wall early afternoon. She hadn't turned up for a drink with him the night he'd had his treatment, and he hadn't pursued it. He didn't want to seem too keen and get her wondering about his motivation.

He'd made a plan, grabbed some hiking gear, and his walking sticks, and—foolishly—only one bottle of water, and headed up the hill towards the rock face at eleven o'clock.

Now four hours later, he was hot, sunburned, cranky and probably dehydrated; honestly this case was doing his head in. Maybe it was time to give up and decide what he was going to do.

Whether he was going to go back and work with Patrick, or if he was going to stay in Australia for a while. Do some travelling and not have to skulk around tailing people who didn't want to be found.

Now it looked as though the one he had been going to "bump" into accidentally this afternoon had changed her mind about climbing the hill, and he'd wasted his time. And got a good dose of sunburn as well.

As Ronan sat there feeling cranky and trying to summon up the energy to move, a small rockfall tumbled down the cliff below him and to his left.

More freakin' goats, he thought. He'd encountered a couple of large feral goats on the track halfway up and they had given him a scare. They were three times the size of the cute goats on his Pa's farm. And not only were they bloody ugly, they were also curious.

He leaned his head back and closed his eyes to summon up the energy to go back down. His head was starting to ache and his vision flickered a bit.

Five more minutes and he'd move. At least when he started off down the track it would be faster than coming up. As long as a bloody goat didn't push him off the path into the sea.

He'd be adding some danger money to his bill this week.

'Jaysus, Mary and bloody Joseph. You're not dead, are you?'

His eyes flew open, and Isla O'Sullivan suddenly appeared in front of him.

'No, I'm not dead. I'm just bloody hot and cranky,' he said before he could think.

She crouched beside him and rocked back on her heels and a cool hand touched his forehead.

'Jaysus, man, you're burning up. Your skin's hotter than Hades. Are you sick? Did you fall?'

He struggled to get up, but a firm hand pushed him back down. 'Stay there while I get my water out.'

'I won't say no to that,' he said with a weak smile.

A minute later a cool bottle of water was thrust into his hand. He unscrewed the lid and put the plastic bottle to his lips.

'Slowly, go slowly,' she said.

'Don't worry, I won't drink all your water. You'll need some too.'

'It's all right. I've got another bottle in my pack.'

As the welcome liquid quenched his thirst, and the bottle cooled his skin, Ronan began to feel better and then realised that here was the perfect opportunity to find out what he needed. Then he could get the hell off this island.

He looked up to encounter a pair of dark eyes full of concern. 'I'm sorry if I gave you a fright. I sat down because I got hot, and I must have drifted off to sleep. And I'm sorry I was a cranky bugger.'

'Feckin' hell, Ronan. I thought you were dead. I was even looking up to see if the vultures were circling.'

'Do you get vultures on a tropical island?'

'I wouldn't know' she said. 'I haven't been here long enough.'

Ronan moved across as Isla sat beside him. There was just enough shade left for both of them.

'Ah, I see. How long have you been here?'

'Are you taking the Mickey out of me?' She looked at him with her eyes that were screwed up to match her forehead.

'Me?' he said. 'What do you mean?'

'We arrived on the same boat, man. So you know exactly how long I've been here.' Her eyes narrowed with suspicion and Ronan cursed inwardly.

Here was his perfect opportunity to do some digging and he was bloody sunstruck and couldn't even get his thoughts in order.

'Ah. I thought you might have been away visiting another island.'

Again, she looked suspicious. 'No. That was the day I moved to the island. Why did you want to know how long I'd been here?'

'No, I just wondered.' His neck heated. 'Sorry, it's none of my business. I'll go back down now and leave you to your walk.'

'Don't be an eejit. You're in no fit state to walk down there by yourself yet. Have some more water, and then we're going to go and sit under that big shady tree.'

'Are you always so bossy? You were quiet and kind when you fixed my back.'

'Ah, so fixed it is, is it? Just as well because walking up that hill wouldn't have done you much good. Especially if you'd slipped on those loose rocks.'

Ronan felt guilty; it had been a ruse to speak to check her out. His injury hadn't been that bad, although the tight muscle in his lower back had been better since the treatment.

'It's been very good. Whatever it was, you fixed it.'

'Well, I'm pleased to be hearing that,' she said. 'Now can you get yourself up, or do I have to help you? We need to get out of this westering sun.'

'I'm fine,' he muttered and put one hand down on the rocky ground to push himself up.

She was nimble and up on her feet before he was, and as she stood beside him, her eyes fixed on him, Ronan's head spun, and he tottered on his feet.

'You're not, you know. Silly man, getting too much sun. What if I hadn't come up and found you? How would it be for the guests to stumble upon a dead Irishman when all they wanted was to see the sun rise over the sea? That would be the end of the island of love, wouldn't it, boyo? Although I suppose it doesn't matter to you, because you are a guest.'

'Do you always talk this much?' he asked as she led him over to the shade.

'Only when I'm trying to stop a silly Irishman from flaking out on me. You've broken the saying, you know.'

'What saying?' He went to shake his head but decided against it as the world tilted.

'Mad dogs and Englishmen. If you'd died up here, it would have been mad dogs and an Irishman. I'm sure Pippa wouldn't have liked that.'

Ronan sat down gingerly, appreciating the shade of the wide spreading tree as she leaned back on the trunk. 'Probably not, although her husband could have written it into a book.'

'Her husband?' She screwed up her face and looked at him. 'What would Rafe be doin' writing that down.'

'Jack Smith.'

Her brow creased in a frown, and she moved closer, peering into his eyes to check if he was delirious or something. 'Look into my eyes, please.'

'He's Jack Smith, *the* Jack Smith who wrote that book that was made into *The Legacy* movie a couple of years ago.'

'Get away with you! Are you sure? You're not dreaming?' She looked at him suspiciously. 'Or pulling my leg because I'm prattling on?'

Ronan couldn't help the smile that tugged at his mouth. He pulled out his phone and was pleased to see he had five bars of service up here. He quickly Googled the book on Amazon and flicked to the second image of the paperback where the author's photo was on the back of the book. He held the phone out. 'Look.'

Before she took it, her eyes widened, and she screeched. 'Jesus, get away from that tree.'

Ronan dropped the phone and scrambled to his feet as she lunged at him and started hitting his shoulders. This time his head didn't spin as he stared at her, and she continued hitting and brushing at his shoulders and neck.

'Is that some sort of beautician treatment for sunstroke?' he asked bemused.

'No, it's me saving you from the army of green tree ants that were marching down your shoulder ready to attack that pink skin on your neck.'

'Jesus!' Ronan lifted the bottom of his T-shirt and pulled it over his head. 'Quick, did you miss any?'

Chapter Twenty-Two

Isla

'No, I think they were only on the outside of your shirt, but there is one in your hair still.' Isla reached up and flicked the almost transparent green and brown ant to kingdom come with her finger.

'And here I was starting to think about emigrating to Australia. I think the bloody feral goats and the giant tree ants have changed my mind. There's a lot to be said for the pouring rain and cold of our Emerald Isle where there's no nasty creatures to disturb a man's peace.'

'Hmph.' Isla couldn't help the nasty sound that escaped her lips before she could stop it. She'd had enough nasty experiences in his Emerald Isle to keep her away from there forever.

He looked at her curiously. 'Not a fan of rain and cold, I guess, then.'

'You could say that. Now sit back down, *away* from that tree trunk, and you can tell me about yourself and why you think Jack Smith lives on the island.' If she was stuck up here on the mountain with him until he was rehydrated, they would talk about him, not her.

He picked up his phone and flicked the screen and handed it to her without a word before he shook his T-shirt vigorously, turned it inside out and then back again, before he pulled it over his head. Once he was finished Isla looked down at the phone and frowned.

'That's Rafe,' she said. 'It *is* Rafe.'

He nodded at her. 'Yes, Pippa's husband, Rafe, is Jack Smith, the famous English author. I read about him moving to some island after I read his second book.'

'Well, I never.' She sat on the grass and looked up at him. 'Sit beside me and drink the rest of that water.'

'Yes, ma'am.' He did as she asked.

'Okay. Now you've told me about Rafe, tell me about yourself, Ronan Doyle. What do you do when you're not having yourself a holiday on an ant-infested goat island.' Isla knew she was in full blather mode but she didn't want to give him the chance to ask her any questions. She figured if she gave him ten minutes or so, and he drank both her bottles of water, he'd be right to get down the hill.

'Me? I'm pretty boring.' He sat close to her, so close that when he moved, his legs brushed against hers. She didn't want to move away and make it look too obvious, but she was still uncomfortable so close to a man, especially one she didn't know.

'What sort of work, do you do?'

'A bit of commercial photography.' He gestured to the camera bag on the ground across from them. She'd been so worried about him she hadn't noticed it before. 'Birds.'

'Commercial bird photography. What does that mean?'

'You know, nature stuff. And landscapes. Tourist brochures and the like. Magazines, ads, all sorts of things.'

'Is there money in it? Enough to live on?' She swallowed a smile as he gawked at her. It was not the done thing to talk about money, but Isla had learned that doing the right thing never got you anywhere.

'Enough to get by.'

'And why do you want to move to Oz?' She tipped her head to the side as she looked at him. He had unusual eyes—flecks of gold in the brown. Very trustworthy eyes.

He stared back and a shiver went through Isla as she saw curiosity in his expression. She rushed on, 'Do you not have family over there? A wife, brothers and sisters that'll miss you.'

'I do have family there,' he replied. 'But they all have their own busy lives. My sister's husband wants me to join up my business with his, but I'm only just startin' to think about it now.' As he spoke, he dropped back into the deep burr of the south west.

'The southwest you said you were from. Even if you hadn't said that I would have picked it from the way you said "goat".'

'Goat? I don't say it any different to you.'

'Yes, you did. One syllable. So, tell me where exactly are you from?'

He shook his head. 'Not from Dublin, like you. I'm from Dingle.'

Isla froze. 'Dingle?'

'What's wrong with me coming from Dingle?'

'You really and truly came from Dingle?'

'I do.'

'Tell me about it.'

'Tell you what?'

'Tell me about Dingle.' Isla had a feeling that Ronan Doyle was telling the truth and she'd run into the only person she'd ever met who came from Dingle. Dingle, the village she'd chosen on the map, as far away from Dublin as she could pick and where she'd pretended she'd grown up, to everyone who had asked about her past over the last nine years.

He looked at her curiously again. 'Well, I was born and grew up in Dingle. I lived there until five years ago when I went to work for—when I changed my career to follow my love of . . . um . . . photography of birds.'

'What sort of birds are there in Dingle?' she asked trying to catch him out. Him coming from Dingle was too much of a coincidence for her peace of mind. Suspicion tinged her tone, but he still held her gaze steadily.

'The Dingle Peninsula is one of the best birdwatching areas in Ireland, and famous for its seabird colonies. My da used to take me birdwatching when I was a little fella. I asked for a camera one Christmas, and I got one. That's where it all started.'

'What sort of birds?' she repeated. He looked at her as though she was the one with sunstroke.

'Okay, there's many different varieties. The Blasket and the Maharee islands together have tens of thousands of nesting birds every summer.'

'What sort, I asked?'

He shook his head. 'Where do I start? Storm petrels, shearwaters, terns, gulls and auks, and the colourful puffins. Before I moved away, I used to work on the eco-marine tours on Blasket Island.'

Isla widened her eyes as relief flooded through her. No one could have made all that up on the spur of the moment. He was telling the truth. It was a coincidence! She couldn't help the laugh that began to bubble up from her chest. 'You really do come from Dingle?'

'I do. That's what I said. What's the joke? It's not that sad a town.'

'How big is your family?

'I have a younger sister and four brothers older than me.'

Isla snorted. 'Tell me their names aren't Paulie, Johnny, Archie and Barrie, please.'

'No,' he said cautiously, looking at her as though she'd well and truly lost the plot. 'Declan, Liam, Tony and Kevin. Why?'

'Did your grandparents live with you?' Isla giggled again. 'And did you go the village school?'

'The village school? Have you never been to Dingle?' he asked. 'It's not a village, and there is no "village" school. My brothers and I went to school in Ballyduff.'

'Well, I got that part wrong,' she said half to herself.

Ronan sat up straight and his gaze was intense. 'Isla, are you feeling all right? What are you talking about?'

'You know, it's an absolute hoot. I've done some serious thinking since I arrived on the island, I'm pretty sure I'm going to settle and make a new life here. An honest one.' She snorted again. 'And who comes along? An Irishman who grew up in feckin' Dingle! I have to tell the girls first that it's been a sham.'

Ronan scratched his head as he kept looking at her. He looked confused—and she couldn't blame him—but there was a flare of interest in his eyes too. The sort of interest she usually ignored or talked over until the guy's eyes glazed over.

'Do you want to tell me what you're talking about,' he asked softly. 'Or do you want me to play a guessing game?'

'No, I'll be honest with you. I think you arriving on Pentecost Island in my first week is a sign.'

'A sign from who? The Almighty?'

'Hell, no! Not *the* Almighty that you're probably talking about. I lost my faith in that one when I stopped being myself.'

He leaned over and put his hand on her arm and she looked down at the long tanned fingers against her still fair skin. 'Look, I'm feeling a lot better now thanks to you rescuing me, and your bottles of water. Before it gets any hotter how about we head back down, grab a couple of beers and find a shady spot and you can tell me your story.'

Isla nodded slowly as he looked at her earnestly, and on a totally out of character impulse, she decided to trust him. 'Yes. I think I'd like that.'

Chapter Twenty-Three
Ronan

Ronan didn't know whether to be excited because he was getting close to wrapping up this job or whether he felt like a total shit. The Isla who had rescued him from the hill, and the Isla of the competent massage treatment was very different to the loudmouthed and brash woman on the boat on the way to the island.

She obviously trusted him and getting up close and personal with her didn't sit comfortably with him in terms of the assignment. The last few jobs he'd completed for clients had not involved speaking to or getting close to the person he was searching for.

Not that he wouldn't like to get up close and personal with Isla O'Sullivan. He enjoyed her company, she had a wicked sense of humour and a quirky turn of phrase, not to mention being one of the most beautiful women he had ever seen. Her dark eyes had an exotic slant to them, and her black hair tumbled past her shoulders in a riot of curls. Her beautiful lips were a natural rosy colour. Even though he's been feeling so woozy up on the hill, he still hadn't been able to take his eyes off her. The photos his client had given him didn't do her justice.

Ronan was caught between a rock and a hard place, and as he walked back to his hut to take a cool shower after he left her at the bottom of the hill, he wondered if he'd done the wrong thing by organising to have a beer with Isla.

He stood under the shower and let the hard jets of cold water soothe his overheated and sunburnt face. As he tipped his head back, he tried to figure out how to approach this. Reaching for the soft white bath sheet he patted his red face dry before digging out some clean clothes.

As he went to lock the door of the hut behind him, he wondered if he should take his camera, so he'd look like a bona fide photographer.

Huh, he thought. This was a drink and chat date; she wouldn't expect him to be working.

Isla was waiting for him at the pool bar where they had organised to meet. She was chatting to a barman he hadn't seen before and when she put her head back and laughed at something the guy said, a flash of jealousy hit Ronan.

How stupid. He had no reason—or right—to feel like that.

'Where's your camera?' Isla asked when he crossed the outdoor area to the bar. 'There's going to be a ripper of a sunset.'

'Ah, I was in too much of rush to meet you.' He stumbled over his words. 'Plus, I thought it was probably rude to bring it.'

She looked at him curiously. 'I wouldn't mind.'

'Okay, I'll get our drinks and I'll collect it and my tripod'—that sounded professional—'on our way. What would you like to drink? A beer or a wine? I'm a lot cooler now.'

'You're nowhere near as red-faced. You had me worried there for a while.' She'd obviously had a quick shower too. Her hair was damp, and the curls were hanging in tight ringlets. 'How about we get a bottle of wine, or are you a beer sort of guy?'

'A cold white wine would be refreshing.' Ronan nodded as the barman passed him the wine list, and he ran his finger down. 'An NZ sauvignon blanc? Is that okay?'

'Sounds good. You grab the wine and I'll get some water and glasses. And maybe some nibbles. Do you have anything here, Larry?'

The barman hadn't taken his eyes off her as she'd chattered away, and he reached down and took out a readymade plate of cheese, olives, and cold meat from the fridge beneath the counter.

'All ready for the evening rush, but you're the first, Isla.' He flicked a glance at Ronan. 'Later tonight after I knock off, how about we have a drink up in the staff quarters?'

The hide of the gobshite, Ronan thought as he gave him a death glare.

'Thanks, Larry, but I have a rule not to socialise with the staff. And I need an early night too. A full day of bookings again tomorrow.'

With a shrug, he grinned. 'Nothing ventured, nothing gained.' Ronan couldn't help looking smug as they left the bar.

Isla led the way to a grassy point on the northern side of the jetty. There were a couple of rustic tables with bench seats overlooking the sea, but there was no one else making use of them.

Ronan opened the bottle of wine and filled the two glasses and passed one over to Isla. She uncovered the plate of cheese and pushed it over to him. 'You're probably hungry after your big adventure. And you forgot to get your camera again.'

He shook his head. 'No, I decided to give my whole attention to you while you tell me your story.'

'Oh.'

'You don't sound as enthusiastic anymore,' he commented.

'I am. It's going to be good to talk about why I am the way I am. Or the way I was. I think it's going to be cathartic for me. Strangers passing in the night. You don't know me, and you won't judge me. I'll stay here on the island, and you'll move onto your next adventure.' Her grin was cheeky as she looked up at him, and again he was stuck by her exotic beauty.

'I guess it was the Dingle connection that did it.'

Isla laughed and put one hand to her chest. She'd changed and was wearing a bright red T-shirt with *Love Hard, Live Longer* on the front. 'It was. I absolutely thought you were taking the Mickey out of me, and you knew what my background was. Or the one I used.'

Ronan picked up his glass and held it up for her to clink hers on. 'Here's to Dingle and old and new pasts, and to a mysterious woman who has crossed my path.'

Her smile was sweet, but there was tension around her pretty eyes.

'So, Isla Sullivan, tell me about the real you. I know you are definitely a massage therapist, because of the awesome job you did on my back. What else are you?'

She reached over and carefully put a piece on cheese on one of the crackers. 'I'll start at the beginning.'

'Always a good place to start.' Ronan immediately knew his tone was too flippant. He reached over and placed his hand on hers. 'I'll listen and I won't judge.'

'Thank you.' Isla stared over his shoulder looking towards the sunset as she began to speak. 'I was born in Dublin almost thirty years ago, into a high achieving family. My name was Isla Aisling O'Sullivan, and I was called Aisling—Ash for short— until I chose to leave. My grandmother's name was Isla and I preferred Aisling then. My da and my mam were both lawyers and I often wondered why they ever had me. All my memories of my childhood were of nannies, and cooks.' She picked up the glass and took a big sip. 'And a mean bully of a big sister. Her name was Marlene, and I haven't seen her for ten years. Or my parents.' Her voice dropped to a whisper. 'And I don't want to.'

Ronan froze. Marlene was the name of his client. Hearing the name of the woman who'd hired him from Isla's lips made him very uncomfortable. Later, he knew that that's when he should have stopped her and told her why he was here, and what he knew, but this afternoon he was transfixed by the look on her face. A combination of sadness and regret, but there was also strength. Her mouth was set in a straight line and her fingers clenched the stem of the wine glass, but Isla continued.

He could tell that she *needed* to talk. Now that she had started, it seemed as though it was hard for her to stop.

'I started high school, and I hit adolescence with a vengeance. All my father—and I guess my mother too—wanted was for another smart daughter, a daughter who would be biddable and follow her sister into the family law firm. I hated the thought of it. The only thing I loved at school were my English lessons, and if I'd gone up to university it would have been to study literature.'

She continued to look past him, and her eyes were sad. 'We'll cut to the year I was supposed to finish my schooling and get my university entry. I thought I was pretty cool.' She turned her gaze to him for a moment. 'I did everything I could to get their attention, but nothing worked. I wagged school, I smoked, I stole money from Da's wallet, it changed nothing.'

She took a deep breath. 'Until one day when I met a man—I guess he would have been a boy, but I was too smitten to take much notice. He loved literature and he understood me.' Her hand shook as she put the glass down. 'At least I thought he did. I guess I saw what I was wanting to see.

'Anyway, to cut a long story short, I fell pregnant, as many Irish girls did in those days. Being good Catholics and all.'

Ronan drew a quick breath and she flicked him an amused glance.

'You think that got my parents' attention?'

He shook his head. 'I guess not, or you wouldn't be here telling me this story.'

'Got it in one, boyo. Now we get to the nasty bit.' She sipped her wine this time. Ronan ignored his glass, he was riveted by her story, and as she spoke, he knew that he would not be completing this job. She had been treated badly, and it wasn't up to him to deliver her to the sister who was looking for her. He would email her tonight, and say he was mistaken about finding her, and terminate the contract.

'My da was still determined I would pass my exams, and he hired a tutor to get me there. I was locked in my room for six hellish weeks with this pervert of a tutor who would arrive every morning and lock the door behind him at night.'

Ronan felt sick as he listened. 'That's against the law.'

'Probably, but all my da wanted was the top exam marks. Marlene topped the school and got the university medal the year she graduated.' Her voice shook as her eyes brimmed with tears. 'I got what I deserved.'

Chapter Twenty-Four

Aisling

'Are you absolutely sure?' The counsellor in the private clinic in London stared at Aisling after her father left the room.

Aisling nodded, unable to bring herself to speak because she knew she'd start crying, and if she started, there would be no stopping her.

She looked up at the counsellor and the nurse sitting across the coffee table from her, where papers sat waiting for her to sign.

'I sensed a tension between you and your father. It is most unusual for a father to bring his daughter to the clinic, so I want to be absolutely sure that it is you who wants this termination, and it's not simply your father's—or your parents'—wishes. The initial consultation is usually done with the patient alone, to make sure she's happy with her decision. Your father was most insistent on coming in with you.'

Aisling dug deep as she stared at the woman's hair. She couldn't bring herself to look at her eyes, and she spoke by rote.

'It is my choice. My parents support me. My father came across to London with me from Dublin as my mother is working on an important case. They are both solicitors, you know.' She swallowed. 'I never knew that we couldn't have an abortion in Ireland. How naïve was I?'

'Not naïve, at all. It's not the sort of thing that an eighteen-year old would pay much attention to. You are aware of the other options?'

'I think so.'

'Now according to your GP who referred you, you are ten weeks pregnant.'

Aisling nodded. She knew the baby was Niall's, but once she had told Da about Sean assaulting her, and the test had indeed confirmed a pregnancy, she had let her parents make the assumption that Sean was the father.

She was tired, distressed and more emotional than she had ever been in her life.

Consumed by hatred, and distress that Niall had not tried to find her, Aisling followed her parents' wishes. She tried very hard not to think about the tiny little thing inside her ever being a person.

'The three choices are abortion, becoming a parent, or adoption.' The nurse's voice was soft, and the kindness in her tone almost brought Aisling to tears.

'I know. That's why we're at the clinic.'

'Very well. If you would just sign here, and here, please Miss O'Sullivan.'

She quickly did as she was told and looked down at her hands clenched on her lap.

'Tomorrow morning, you will be placed under a general anaesthetic and the procedure will only take ten to fifteen minutes,' the nurse continued. 'Most women don't experience any problems after this procedure. But there are some risks, such as infection of the womb, damage to the womb and excessive bleeding. We will give you painkillers and an aftercare phone line so you can call us any time of the day or night if you are worried.'

'When are you going back to Dublin?' the counsellor asked.

Aisling lifted her head, and her steely determination kicked in. 'I'm not.'

##

Two days later, Aisling stood outside the private clinic beside her father.

He insisted that she come home with him, but despite her weak physical condition and her confused emotional state, she had found the strength to stand up to him.

'I will never set foot in that house again. Not after what happened there in *my* bedroom. It is all on your head.' She couldn't even bring herself to say *Da.*

'Now, now,' he'd huffed as he'd tried to get her into the Jag. 'Don't be like that. I'll admit that I was wrong.'

Aisling's laugh was bitter as she pushed away his hand.

'But that is in the past now. We've sorted it out—'

'Have we?' she finally yelled. 'How have we done that?'

'Sean Roberts will never work in teaching again, and medically we've got you sorted.'

Bile rose in her throat at her father's attitude. 'I'm so pleased for your peace of mind that you have me all "sorted" in your head.' She fought back the tears that were always there. She would not cry in front of her father. 'Goodbye. Have a nice life.'

Chapter Twenty-Five

Isla

'What did you do?' Somehow Ronan had moved around to her side of the table and his arms were around her, and her head was resting on his shoulder. Isla blinked, surprised to feel her cheeks wet. She had blocked the thought of those two days, and the following weeks for a long time.

'I waited until he was in the car and went to his window. I held my hand out and told him I wanted money. He must have known I was serious because he pulled his wallet out. Before he opened it, he looked at me and his eyes were like flint.

'"If you take this, you will no longer be our daughter," he said to me. "It is the last I will ever give you. You have been a constant disappointment to your mother and I, your whole life."'

'Jaysus!' Ronan's voice vibrated against her cheek. 'What the hell did you do?'

'He gave me five hundred pounds, and I was still clutching it in my hand when I was taken to emergency. Someone found me crying in the gutter, and I was incoherent. I spent six weeks in a mental health ward. I'm not proud to say I had a total breakdown; it took me five years to get my self-confidence back. When I was in hospital, I would sit in the garden and invent the family I wanted to have.' She lifted her head and smiled through her tears. 'My Dingle family. All my lovely brothers and my parents and my grandparents. For a while there, they all became very real to me.'

'If you had really been in Dingle, I would have been your friend, Isla.' His eyes held hers and they were full of kindness. 'What about the father of your baby? The boy you met?'

Her laugh was bitter. 'I found Niall on Facebook a few years back. He's a tutor at Trinity now, and he has a lovely wife and two young children. I wonder if he ever thinks of the girl he thought of as one of his Thomas Hardy heroines?'

'What about your sister? Were you ever in contact with her?'

'No, but I keep tabs on her through Facebook. She's married now and has her own law firm.'

'You wouldn't ever want to talk to her, or your parents?'

'No. I don't have any family. Or rather I choose not to. I realise that it wasn't my fault. I was a normal teenager, and I was treated very badly. My life is my own, and I am going to make it a good life.' She reached out and took Ronan's hand. 'Thank you so much for listening to me. I'm very pleased you chose Pentecost Island for your holiday. You were meant to pass through my life.'

To her surprise he looked quite distressed, and he moved away from her and then stood suddenly.

'Do you mind if I leave you here for a few minutes? Please don't go, but there is something I have to do. Would you like me to bring anything back? More wine? Or how about I order some dinner at the bar?'

She nodded. 'That would be good, thank you. Pizza?'

Even though she smiled up at him, Ronan looked very serious, and she wondered if she had gone too far, telling her life story to a stranger.

'Pizza, it is. Give me ten minutes.'

As Isla watched Ronan stride across the grass towards the path laughter drifted down from Pippa and Rafe's house, making her smile. An unfamiliar feeling of lightness had descended on her when she had shared her story with Ronan. He had been very kind to her, and she had to admit that when his arms had gone around her, it had felt right.

****

Ronan cursed himself in all manner of ways as he hurried back to his hut. How the hell did this get so complicated? He detoured via the bar and ordered two medium pizzas, and another bottle of wine from a sour Larry, but he didn't give a shit about that guy's problem. All he was focused on was getting back to his laptop and sending an email off to

England to his client—Isla's bloody sister. The one who had treated her like dirt.

After hearing what Isla had been through Ronan didn't want anything to do with this job anymore. He pulled out his laptop, powered it up and connected to the Wi-Fi and thought carefully about the wording of his email.

In the end he kept it brief and formal.

Dear Marlene

Please note that I was mistaken in identifying the woman I emailed you about as your sister. That person is not Aisling O'Sullivan. I apologise for my error. As the trail seems to be cold I will now remove myself from this assignment. There is no account outstanding. Thank you for your patience. I am sorry that I could not assist you. Sincerely, Ronan Doyle.

Listening to Isla's story had been harrowing. He could not comprehend that a family—a mother and father—could treat their child as she had been treated. Granted, she had made mistakes, but they should have supported her. Trying to relate to how parents could be like that was impossible for him. His parents and his siblings would have been supportive and caring.

With a disgusted shrug, he composed himself and after he pressed send, he locked the door behind him and headed back to the beach where he had left Isla.

He was surprised to see Pippa and Rafe standing at the table and hurried across hoping that everything was okay. He was reassured when he heard Isla's distinctive laugh.

'Hi there,' he said. 'How did the wedding go?'

Pippa's smile was wide. 'It was beautiful We've just taken Nell and Nat down to the wharf to Rafe's boat. We were on our way back when we noticed Isla sitting here.'

Isla turned to him. 'Pippa and Rafe gave the happy couple a week in a penthouse on Hamilton Island.'

Pippa shook her head. 'As grateful as they were, would you believe that Nell said she'd rather be here on the island!'

Isla chuckled. 'It is known as the island of love.'

'There's no way I'd let them spend their wedding week in the staff lodge! The huts are at full capacity for the next two months.'

Ronan pulled a face. 'I was hoping to extend my stay, but it looks as though that won't be possible.'

'Actually, I was going to come and see you tomorrow,' Pippa said. 'Tess told me that Zac told her—nothing like the island grapevine—that you're a commercial photographer.'

'He is,' Isla exclaimed. 'He's done work for magazines and brochures promoting Dingle in southwest Ireland.'

Ronan nodded. 'I am and I have.' He flicked a smile to Isla, pleased that she sounded so upbeat now.

'Do you have a portfolio I could look at?' Pippa pulled a face at Rafe. 'I know. It's not work time, but you know me, when I get an idea, I'm ready to run with it.'

Her husband put his arm around her and dropped a kiss on top of her head. 'I know and I wouldn't have you any other way, love.'

'I have a digital portfolio. I can give you the link.'

'Great, send it to the email address in your compendium,'—she patted the pockets of her dress—'I don't carry a business card in my wedding finery.'

'What sort of photography are you looking for?'

'A bit of everything, but mainly up at Red Wave Wall, and up in the hills. We're looking at really developing the climbing and birdwatching market.'

Ronan caught Isla's eye and could see the mirth on her face. He put a hand on her shoulder.

'Don't you say a word, Ms O'Sullivan.'

'My lips are sealed,' she said with a giggle.

Pippa looked from Ronan to Isla and a satisfied smile lit up her face. 'Sounds like you two Irish are hitting it off. Good to see.'

Rafe tugged at his wife's hand. 'As much as we'd love to stay and chat, we still have about twenty guests up at the house. Good to catch up with you both. Have a good evening.'

They walked off together towards the step leading up to the house on the top of the hill and as Ronan turned back, Isla put one hand to her chest.

'Oh my God, now I know he's Jack Smith too, I'm even more smitten.'

'He seems like a nice guy. Hey, and thanks for the photography plug too.'

'My pleasure. As long as you remember to wear sunscreen and take water with you if you get the assignment. And I'm sure you will. Get it, I mean. Pippa seemed pretty keen before you came back.'

'She hasn't seen any of my work, and besides, there's nowhere to stay. I can't extend my booking.' Ronan tried not to get excited about the possibility of a job with the island.

'I'm sure she'll figure something out.'

He held his hand out to pull Isla up from the bench seat. 'Now before you go puttin' the cart in front of the horse, *macushla*, we have two pizzas to eat, and wine to drink. Are you ready?'

'I am. Are we going to eat at the bar?'

'If you're happy to.'

'Yes. As long as you and Larry don't look daggers at each other. It might ruin my appetite.'

Ronan laughed as he pulled her up. 'How about you take it as a compliment. And Isla?'

'Yes?' Those beautiful dark eyes held his.

'I am so pleased to see you smiling. That was a big story you told me before.'

'Thank you for listening.' Before he realised what she intended, soft lips brushed his cheek. 'I really appreciated it. I feel so good. Now I'm starving, let's go eat.'

Ronan smiled as she held his hand all the way back to the bar.

Chapter Twenty-Six

Pippa -Three weeks later

I dressed quickly, came out of the medical rooms, and hurried across to Rafe who was waiting in the foyer. He'd been in the room with me when the sonographer held the wand thing on my bare tummy, and he had held my gaze as we both heard the rapid little heartbeat. Excitement had taken over when the obstetrician had met with us and confirmed that not only was the baby fine and growing quickly, but I was four weeks out in my dates, and was a month further along than I thought.

Our baby was due in late winter. And by then, we would have four babies on the island.

Rafe put his arm around my shoulders as we walked to the car he kept in an underground garage near the marina at Port of Airlie. Neither of us said a word until we were heading along Shute Harbour Road.

I put both hands up to my face, and Rafe glanced over at me, and then put his hand on my knee. 'We've been given a gift of four weeks, Rafe. I can't believe it. Four weeks when I didn't have to worry about reaching the twelve-week mark, and now we're there.'

'I couldn't believe it when the doctor said that.'

'And everything is going perfectly and he's really happy. Do you think I'll be tempting fate if I'm a little bit happy too?'

'A little bit happy?' He shook his head. 'No, we are both going to let ourselves be very happy. Not only happy, but . . . ecstatic. Overjoyed. Thrilled. Elated and—'

'Okay, stop showing off, Mr Author,' I said as he turned the car off the roundabout leading to the apartment block where the car was garaged.

I put my hand on my stomach and looked down. 'He sure had a strong little heartbeat, didn't he?'

'*She* sure did,' Rafe said with a chuckle. 'And she looked very comfortable all curled up inside you.' He parked the car and came around to my side and opened the door. 'Now that we're past twelve weeks, can we break the news?'

I nodded. 'First thing we'll do as soon as we get back.'

'Great timing because everyone's home.'

'Jed and Evie too?' I linked my arm through his as we walked to his boat.

'Yes, Jed called when you were getting changed. They're on the way over now with the new furniture for the top glade.'

'Oh, that's fabulous. And Zac and Tess came back last night, and Philippe and Eliza sailed around the point as we were heading across the Passage this morning.' I leaned into him. 'But I think there's one call you should make before we tell everyone.'

He looked down at me and squeezed my fingers. 'You don't mind?'

'Of course not, and as soon as we tell everyone Odessa will be on the phone to Jenny and Bryant, so you need to call them first.'

'How about now? As soon as we get on the boat?' He glanced at his watch. 'We should just catch them before they retire for the night.'

I giggled. 'Have I told you how much I love you today, Rafe?'

'Not in the last half hour.' He leaned down and caught me in a kiss. 'You have been very remiss.'

'As you would be *remiss* if you didn't catch them before they *retired for the night*.'

He kissed me again to stop me giggling.

'Okay, I shall do the right thing and ring them before they go to bed, you wench. You do realise that I shall be teaching our daughter to speak properly. None of this casual Aussie lingo.'

'Oh, will you just?' I nudged him with my shoulder and received another kiss.

As soon as we were on Rafe's boat, he called Jenny and Bryant, and the joy on his face as he broke our news to his best friends in England had me blinking away happy tears.

##

Our island was buzzing when we walked from the wharf to the office. We'd decided on the way back it would be too hard to get everyone together, so we decided to call in and deliver our news to everyone wherever they happened to be as we walked around the resort.

The last three weeks had seen some changes at Ma Carmichael's. Nell had dropped back to three hours a day in the office. Eliza was working with the Riccardos on the design of the new accommodation up the hill for the birdwatching and climbing groups and was more often than not in the office with Tess using the computers. The renovations of Aunty Vi's house were almost complete, and I couldn't believe how fast the builder's crews worked.

They were about to start work on the new buildings up past the staff lodge, and I had hired Ronan Doyle as our onsite photographer, both for advertising photos, as well as to record images for the development of the resort. Isla had given me the idea when she mentioned in passing one day that Esculanta Island had a history montage of photographs in the main restaurant. I'd managed to dig out a lot of Aunty Vi's old photos too. I smiled to myself as I remembered how pleased Isla had been when she had heard that Ronan was staying on the island for a while and moving into a room up at the staff lodge. They seemed to have developed a strong friendship over the past month, and I often saw them walking along the shore in the early evening.

As we approached the house I paused and looked around. 'I wonder what Aunty Vi would have made of all this?' I said to Rafe.

'She had no doubt that you would live here— she told me that on more than one occasion—but I don't know that she ever thought that you'd turn it into one of the most sought-after resorts in the country. And trust me, she'd be delighted with what you achieved, Pip. You were like a daughter to her.'

'She was a good old stick.' I looked up to the verandah. There was a group sitting at the table on the verandah facing the sea.

'Oh look, we're in luck.' The butterflies in my tummy fluttered with anticipation. 'Nell and Tam are having lunch with Tess and Eliza.'

'And there's Evie and Cherry walking across to the house.'

'Oh yay! And Odessa will be in the boutique too. There's only Sienna and Isla missing.'

'I'm feeling rather outnumbered here. Do you want me to go and you can tell the girls?'

'No. You're coming too. But sweetie, will you go and get Odessa to come out before we tell them, please?'

He ran up the steps ahead of me to the new resort boutique that Odessa had taken over. As well as her handcrafted jewellery, we were stocking some gorgeous sarongs and scarves created by a local designer over on Hamo. It seemed to be a first stop for a lot of the guests as soon as they checked in. And

Odessa had turned out to be an incredible salesperson.

'Hey, Pip. What are you pair up to? A romantic lunch? I thought you went over to Hamo this morning,' Nell said leaning back in her chair. My eyes dropped to the hand she placed on her pregnant stomach, before I moved my gaze to Tamsin. She was sitting on one of the sofas against the wall. She seemed to be bigger every day. Since she'd found out she was carrying twins Tam had stopped working in the catering side of things. Angus had taken over all the ordering and the accounts and was going well.

'No,' I said slowly, making a huge effort not to put my hand on my stomach too. Not that there was any bump there yet, although Rafe said this morning that he could see a little rise, low on my tummy. I had stood at the mirror front on, and side on and twisted from side to side until Rafe chuckled.

'We have some news.'

Tam's eyes narrowed and she nudged Nell who smiled and nodded.

Eliza moaned. 'Not more new buildings?'

Evie looked up from the drawings she had put on the table before she'd sat down. 'More gardens?'

'A new computer system?' Tess asked.

'Another restaurant?' Cherry said hopefully.

Odessa walked out of the boutique with Rafe. She leaned on the wall next to the door and her smile was wide. I raised my eyebrows at Rafe, and he shook his head.

'It wasn't me. Jenny and Bryant called Odessa,' he said.

'What's going on, Pippa?' Tamsin's smile was hopeful.

I couldn't keep the smile from my face as I stood there. 'Well, there's no new buildings, Eliza, and sorry, Cherry, you won't get your own restaurant yet. Evie, no, not gardens. And Tess, we just put in a new computer system, didn't we?'

Rafe walked across to me and put his arm around my shoulders. 'What my darling wife is trying to tell you all, is that in spring, there will be a new addition to Pentecost Island. We're having a baby.'

You never would have guessed that Tam and Nell were pregnant; they both jumped out of their chairs and ran over to me.

I couldn't help myself. I burst into tears as they hugged me and was instantly a blubbering mess.

Tam never cried, but when she spoke her voice trembled. 'Hey, Pip. All for one, and one for all, hey?'

'You got it, sister,' Nell said, joining in the three-way hug.

A flurry of kisses and congratulations followed and eventually Rafe passed me his handkerchief. As I wiped my eyes, I looked at the group of women who were making the island the wonderful place it was, and who I did love as sisters. 'Thanks, everyone. We're pretty excited. Come on, Rafe. We'll go over to *Hebe*, now.' I shook my head. 'We didn't expect to find you all here.'

We left the excited buzz of conversation behind as we headed though the forest to the day spa hut.

'They're probably both in appointments,' I said as we approached *Hebe*.

'It's only ten minutes before the hour so they should be free soon.'

Rafe was right and soon Sienna and Isla knew our news as well.

Isla waited until we were about to leave, and she looked nervous as she spoke to me quietly. 'Pippa, could I come and see you when we finish this afternoon?'

'Sure, come on up to the house. We'll be there.'

'Thanks. I'll see you later.'

Rafe waited for me at the top of the stairs. 'May I take you out for a celebratory lunch now, Mrs Rendell.'

'You may.'

He took my hand, and we walked through the glade together.

Chapter Twenty-Seven

Isla

Isla pounded on Ronan's door. His room was at the other end of the staff lodge from hers. She'd hurried back from her last appointment because they had a sunset date, that is if you could call racing up to the top of the mountain with him a date. Over the past two weeks since Ronan had moved out of the guest accommodation and taken a three-month contract on Pentecost Island to produce a whole new range of brochures for Pippa, Isla had spent most afternoons with him in various locations on the island—including underwater, clad in a head-to-toe stinger suit as he took photos of green turtles.

'Ronan, if you don't get a move on, you're going to miss the light.' She pounded on the door again.

'Okay, okay, I'm coming.' He opened the door and stood there, water running down his bare chest and his hair slicked back. 'I just have to get dressed. Can you come in and grab my camera bag, and check the batteries are in there? And the tripod,' he called over his shoulder as he disappeared into the bathroom.

Isla shook her head as she went inside. One thing she'd discovered about Ronan over the past few weeks was that he had no sense of time.

'Sheesh,' she yelled after his departing back. 'I'm the one who's been at work all day, and what have you been doing? Sitting at the computer, I'd say.'

His head appeared around the door. 'I have, and wait till you see those underwater photos we got last weekend. They are bloody incredible.' He burst out laughing. 'Especially the one of you in your elegant stinger suit.'

'Ronan, hurry up!' She checked the batteries were both there, and then looked at her phone. 'We have fourteen minutes to get up the hill.'

'I'm ready,' he raced out pulling a T-shirt over his wet hair. 'Can you see my thongs?'

'They're out on the veranda.'

'Okay, let's go.'

Isla grinned as she hurried down the steps after Ronan. She'd had the best few weeks since she had spilled her guts to Ronan that night.

They were good mates, as Pippa would say.

'Oh, feckin' hell.' She stopped dead at the bottom of the stairs.

'What's wrong?'

'I totally forgot I arranged to see Pippa at five.'

'Should you go now?' Ronan hoisted the camera bag higher on his shoulder and held his hand out for the tripod she was carrying.

'No. It's a bit late. I said straight after work. I'll leave it until tomorrow. If I'm going to lose my job, one day's not going to make a difference.'

His eyes widened. 'Lose your job? Why?'

'Keep going, we can talk on the way up.'

'What happened?' Ronan asked when they started walking again.

'Nothing. I'm just a bit worried because I'm in my sixth week here, and there's been no mention of permanency or a contract. I was on four weeks probation, and Pippa hasn't mentioned a thing, so I took matters into my own hands and asked her if I could see her this afternoon, and then I forgot all about it. It's your fault.'

'My fault? How can it be my fault?'

'You and your sunsets. I was worried that you'd get involved in your graphics program and you'd lose track of the time and miss this afternoon. You said it was special because the yacht race is on, and the sails with the sun setting would be an awesome shot.'

'Okay. My fault. I can live with that. You're very good to me, Isla.'

'I'm good *for* you. You're starting to learn what a clock is for.'

'Come on then, let's pick up the pace. You're right, they are going to be great shots. The light is perfect already. And don't worry about Pippa and our contract. She loves you, and she probably didn't give it a thought because she's so busy with everything else.'

'And the baby,' Isla added.

'What baby?'

'Didn't you hear? You must be the only one on the island who doesn't know. Pippa and Rafe are having a baby.'

'That's great news.' Ronan stopped as they reached the first gap above Indian Head. 'The island is a great place, isn't it. I'll be sorry to leave. It's worked its magic on me. I've never been so relaxed.'

'And I've never felt this happy. Ever I don't think.'

The look that Ronan flicked her way was hard to fathom. They'd spent hours together in her time off, and the thought of him not being here made her feel strange. Just good mates, no hint of anything else.

For the first time in her life, Isla felt comfortable in her own skin. She was herself and not trying to be anybody else, and every day was a discovery for her as she relaxed and let herself be natural.

The problem was, being relaxed, and letting down her guard, she had let feelings creep in, and that was going to make it hard when Ronan did move on.

Never in a trillion years would she give him any sign that she was interested in him in *that* way.

That would be a sure-fire way to lose him as a friend. He'd be embarrassed. He was a good man, and a good friend, and she would make the most of that while he was here.

When he left, she'd fill the gap somehow.

When she looked up, he was still looking at her and she handed the tripod to him. 'Sorry, I was miles away.'

'Don't worry about your job, *macushla*. I'm one hundred percent sure you have nothing to worry about.' He put his camera bag down, came a step closer, took the tripod from her, and put it on the ground beside the bag.

Tipping his finger beneath her chin he tilted her head up. 'Give me a smile.'

'You'll miss the sunset.'

'There'll be another one tomorrow. You're more important. You look sad. What else is bothering you?'

'Take your photos here and I'll tell you when we get to the top of the path.' Heat ran up from Isla's chest; he stood so close she could feel the warmth of his body against hers.

He flicked her cheek with his finger and smiled. 'Good.'

Within seconds the camera was on the tripod, and the continuous click of the shutter filled the air.

Isla sat on a flat rock and watched as Ronan repositioned the camera a few times. The sun was still well above the mountains and the yachts were still a good distance from the island, but Ronan seemed happy enough. As he focused on the viewfinder, she let her gaze run over his body. He had a stocky build, and he was strong. When he'd held her close that one time, as she'd told him of her past, Isla had felt the corded muscles beneath his shirt, and as she got to know him better, she'd heard about his teenage years spent working on the family farm in Dingle.

A smile crossed her face. *Dingle.*

As she sat there grinning, all was quiet, and she realised that the camera noise had stopped. Ronan was looking at her, and a jolt ran through her as she saw the hunger in his gaze. He looked away quickly and picked up the tripod.

'Come on, let's get to the top of the hill. The yachts will be close enough just in time.' His voice was a bit gruff.

Feckin' hell, now I'm imagining things. Wishful thinking, girl. Get over it.

Chapter Twenty-Eight
Ronan

Spending so much time with Isla, and being close to her was doing Ronan's head in. The more time he spent with her the harder it was to keep his distance. After what she'd been through, and how she'd opened up to him, the last thing he wanted to do was destroy the trust between them.

He would be her friend no matter how hard it was. Leaving Isla at the end of the three months, when he'd completed his contract here was something he tried not to think about.

The crest of the hill appeared ahead, and Ronan paused to let her catch up. She seemed to be in a strange mood this afternoon, but he put that down to her worry about her job.

He had no doubt she was worrying needlessly, but after having watched her over the last few months in various locations, he knew that if anything did happen here, she'd be sure to move on and settle in somewhere else. There was only one thing worrying him. It had been a few weeks since he'd emailed her sister, and there'd not been a reply from her. He was hoping it was because she'd accepted what he'd said and was looking elsewhere.

Isla caught up to him, barely out of breath after the long climb. 'How's the light?'

'Almost there. Come and sit for a while, and you can tell me what else you're worrying about.'

Her teeth flashed in the fading light as she cracked a big grin at him. 'What are you now, my father confessor?'

He nudged her with his shoulder. 'If you have something to confess, I can be.'

'Nope. I never did like going to confession anyway.'

'Come and sit over here, while I set up the remote, then the camera can do its own work while we talk.'

She followed him to the edge of the cliff and sat away from the edge while he secured the tripod, screwed the camera to the top and set it to remote.

He walked over and sat beside her and opened the app on his phone that would control the camera. 'Okay, all set. Now tell Father Ronan what's bothering you. I know something is.'

Isla looked down and wouldn't meet his eyes, and a horrible thought gripped him.

'Jaysus, is it because you don't want to be up here? Am I presuming too much expecting you to traipse around after me after you've been at work all day?'

'Hell no. I totally enjoy being with you.' Finally, she looked up. 'If I'm going to be honest, maybe too much. I'm getting used to you bein' around and when you go, I'm going to miss you.'

Relief flooded though him. 'You'll miss me?'

'I will.'

Ronan leaned back and lifted the phone and pressed the shutter button on the app as the first of the yachts slipped in the golden glow of the sunset.

'Beautiful,' he said. 'Every time I see that photo, I'll think about you missing me. You know what? If you didn't get your contract renewed, it wouldn't be a bad thing. You could come with me. I need a camera assistant.'

Her laugh was soft. 'That's a consolation, anyway.'

As she stared up at him, Ronan forgot all about the yachts and the sunset. Her eyes held his and her lips were softly parted, and he reached out and cupped her cheek. 'And if your contract does get renewed, I might only go as far as Hamilton Island, and then I could see you on weekends. What would you say about that?'

Her lips tilted in a little smile. 'I would say that was an excellent idea.'

'Ah, and what would you say about this?' He leaned forward and touched his lips to hers. The feel of Isla's soft rosy lips beneath his was everything Ronan had dreamed about for the past few weeks. She turned her head slightly and the gentle slide of her moist lips sent need rushing through him. She gripped his T-shirt and held him close. 'I would say that's another excellent idea. There's only one problem.' Her lips vibrated beneath his as she spoke.

'A problem?' he asked.

'The photos.'

'They can wait. This can't. I love touching you.' He slipped his hands beneath her T-shirt and was pleased to hear her moan softly. 'Your lips are like honey and your skin is like silk. You've been in my dreams since the first time I saw you.'

'Do you think we should pack the gear up and go back down to your room. It might be a bit embarrassing for any birdwatcher or rock climber to come across you without your shirt on.'

Ronan frowned and looked down. 'But I've still got my shirt on.'

'Not for much longer, boyo,' she said with a sultry smile.

Chapter Twenty-Nine
Isla

There were degrees of happiness, and Isla realised the next morning, as she sat on the side of Ronan's bed, that she had only scratched the surface over the past few weeks. The feeling that consumed her now was hard to define but it was one she didn't want to let go.

Ronan rolled over and sat up so that he was beside her on the edge of the bed. He yawned. 'What are you doing?'

'Ah, so you're finally awake.'

'That I am,' he said stretching his arms above his head. 'Although, I could do with a bit more sleep.'

'You can sleep after you feed me. I'm going to take a shower while you get me some food, and then you can sleep the day away while I work.'

'Are you really hungry? We had bacon and eggs at midnight!'

'I'm starving again. All that strenuous activity.' She looked at him through half-closed lids and moved away as he went to put his arms around her.

'As much as I'd love to stay, I have to go to work. My first appointment is at eight-thirty. I have forty-five minutes.'

'Okay. I'll go cook you a big breakfast while you shower.' Ronan climbed out of bed and pulled on a pair of jeans.

'You're a good man.'

He came back to her and leaned down and kissed her thoroughly. 'Hold that thought.'

Five minutes later, Isla was showered and dressed. All she had to do was go via her room and put on her *Hebe* uniform.

She crossed the room to the small table where the dishes from their midnight feast sat congealed with remnants of egg and bacon fat. Ronan's camera was sitting on the table, and she picked it up while she waited for him.

If the photo of her in the stinger suit was as awful as he'd said, she'd delete it. Flicking the screen to play, she scrolled through the photos. The one he'd captured last night of the yachts in the golden sunlight was spectacular. Hitting the back button she scrolled though some photos and realised she was going the wrong way. As she went to scroll forward again to search for the turtle photos, her breath caught.

Confusion filled Isla as she looked at photos of herself. Photos of her at the lodge in Alaska. She frowned and kept scrolling. A photo of her at the blues bar in Mission Beach a few months ago. Another photo of her on Esculanta Island, with half of Sienna's face in the background.

What. The. Hell.

The creep, the lowlife bastard.

And she'd fallen for it.

Ronan Doyle from Dingle. Just another man she couldn't trust. And she'd spilled her guts to him.

Isla knew she was going to have to run again. He'd been sent to find her. That was the only reason he'd have photos of her all over the world.

What a fool she'd been to think Ronan was any different to every other man who had been in her life.

It was hard to say whether it was anger or disappointment that was making her hands and legs shake.

She had to get out of here. She had to get off the island. She had to run from the man she loved.

Dropping the camera on the table, not caring if it broke, she grabbed her bag and ran for the door.

***

Ronan was fully awake now, so he'd ended up cooking himself a feed too. It hadn't taken any longer to cook for two, than for Isla. He sang along with the radio as he'd stood at the stove flipping the eggs and waiting for the toast to come up.

Dylan walked in and opened the fridge. 'You're sounding chirpy this morning, Ronan.' His glance was knowing. 'Had a good night, did you?'

Ronan flicked him a look. 'A good night?'

'Yeah, I just saw a certain pretty Irish girl sneak out of your room. She was in a hurry; she took off like a rocket.'

Ronan frowned and switched the stove off. 'Where to? She hasn't had her breakfast yet.'

Dylan poured a glass of milk and then drank it before he shrugged. 'I thought Isla must have been late for work, because she went down the steps really fast.'

Ronan lifted the pan onto the table and quickly transferred the toast to one plate, and then tipped the eggs on. 'Have a good day,' he said as he hurried from the kitchen wondering where Isla had gone.

Maybe she'd had second thoughts, although she'd been a willing participant all night.

With a frown he headed back to his room, carrying the plate of eggs and toast.

Chapter Thirty
Isla

By the time Isla reached the spa hut, she had her emotions under a semblance of control. Her anger was bubbling under the surface, and she knew she was going to have to work very hard to keep it under control.

She wasn't going to run from Pentecost Island. As crazy as it was, even though she knew that Ronan wasn't who he had pretended to be, he had still helped her face her demons.

She drew in a shaky breath as she unlocked the door and went inside.

And he had turned out to one of her demons. Another man who had proved he couldn't be trusted.

But she no longer had any fear of the past. Her first thought was that Ronan had been following her to get information for her father. Although she couldn't understand why it had taken almost ten years for him to look for her. Even if her father turned up here, she was a grown woman heading for thirty, for feck's sake. And why would he anyway? Da had made it quite clear that she was no longer his daughter or a member of their family.

And that suits me just fine.

It was hard to hold in her emotions as she thought of the way her parents had treated her when she was eighteen. Locked away with a man who had turned out to be untrustworthy, her parents then forced her to have an abortion and then Da had abandoned her on a street in London. It was unforgivable. If they *had* sent someone to find her and bring her home, they—and bloody Ronan Doyle—could go take a flying leap.

Her second thought was that Ronan was some sort of creepy stalker, but she dismissed that as soon as the possibility came to her. Before she knew that he had been secretly taking photographs of her, she'd got to know him, and she'd liked him. More than liked him, if she was honest. She would have preferred it if he had asked her outright why she was here, rather than gradually gaining her trust and finding out about her dishonestly.

With a sigh, Isla crossed to the desk. That wasn't quite true, because if he had simply asked her about her past, for sure she would have given him the whole happy family spiel.

But she'd foolishly trusted him and opened her heart and soul to him and told him the truth. Stuff she'd never told anyone before.

Not even Sienna.

If he'd been any sort of decent and honest human being, he would have told her then that he already knew all about her, and why he was here. If he'd been honest, maybe she could have tried to understand.

But, no.

Instead, he'd reached out and held her, and for feck's sake, she'd burrowed into his shoulder and lapped the attention up like a needy child.

Well, never again. That just showed her what happened when she took down her barriers and trusted someone.

As Isla's anger faded, disappointment kicked in. She'd really *liked* Ronan, and she'd just spent the night in his bed. An incredible night, and she was sure she had seen the true Ronan, either that or he was a bloody good actor.

As she crossed the room, she spotted a note on the reception desk in Sienna's loopy writing.

'Tess called. Your nine-thirty has cancelled, but now you have a ten-thirty after that. Hut Seven, but I didn't catch the name.'

As Isla prepared the room for her first client, she tried to push Ronan from her thoughts.

Deep breaths, think of good things. The psychologist in the mental health ward in London had taught her those strategies, and she'd tried to practise them every time the blackness descended.

For the first few years, it had been hard to think of good things. As Isla had travelled the world, she had banked a store of beautiful images in her mind and was able to run them through her thoughts like a slide show when she needed to. The huge lemons on the trees growing on the steep hills on the Amalfi coast, the beautiful untouched canvas of blinding-white snow around the lodge in Alaska, the faces of the beautiful children in Bali; the images and memories always calmed her.

Closing her eyes, she tried to summon the scenes to her thoughts, but all she could see were the photos on Ronan's camera, and her anger came rushing back.

Why? Why had he let her down too? Like everyone else did. Why did he have to be the same?

Isla wondered if he'd come looking for her, or if he'd stay away from her now that she was on to him. He'd noticed the camera had been moved, and he'd realise she'd seen the photos on it.

She didn't care what Ronan's reaction was; he couldn't be trusted to tell the truth. She couldn't trust him. She was incapable of trust.

As Isla stood at the window, her hands clenched by her side, Sienna opened the door and walked in with a wide smile.

'Good morning, you look tired, *liebling*. Did you have a late night?'

'Have you been talking to Dylan?' Isla couldn't help her snappish reply.

'No? Should I have?' Sienna's smooth brow creased in a frown and guilt trickled though Isla. It wasn't Sienna's fault.

'Sorry I was short tempered. I'm tired.' Isla closed her eyes briefly. She felt as though anyone who looked at her today would know she'd spent the night in Ronan's bed. She looked up and cleared her throat. 'What about Ronan? Was he there?'

'I didn't see him; I was only to have a quick piece of toast and a coffee. Are you okay? You don't look very happy.' Her voice held concern. 'What's wrong?'

'I'm not very happy at all, but don't worry. I won't let my bad mood impact on the clients today. I'm going to go over and see Pippa after the first appointment.'

Sienna's frown deepened. 'Tell me what's wrong, Isla. You're not thinking about leaving the island, are you?'

'No. I won't do that. If I did, I'd let you know first.'

'Good. I was worried for a moment.' Sienna moved towards the door and hesitated. 'You know, Isla, if there's anything you need to talk about, I'm happy to listen.'

A lump rose in Isla's throat as she heard the sympathy in her friend's voice.

'Thank you.' She unclenched her fingers and tried to relax. 'I appreciate that. But I'm all good. I'll get over it. And I won't let you down.'

'Okay, but I have offered that I am here if you would like to talk. Remember that.'

'I will.'

'Isla? I wanted to—' Sienna hesitated and then opened the door to her treatment room. 'It doesn't matter. I'll talk to you later.' She closed the door quietly behind her, and Isla frowned, wondering what she had been going to say.

With a shrug, she began to prepare for her first client. There was a clean uniform in the cupboard in her treatment room, and once she had changed, she lit the candles on the bench under the window. With a deep sigh, Isla looked out the window, and wondered why her life had gone to shite again.

Worst of all, she knew was going to miss Ronan like crazy, the Ronan she thought she'd knew. Not the lowlife, conniving, dishonest man he really was.

Chapter Thirty-One

An hour later, Isla had one satisfied client leave the treatment room.

'Best hot stone massage I've ever had. You've got good hands, love.'

'Thank you. We aim to please here on Pentecost Island.' She managed to keep her voice upbeat, and she smiled as the woman left a hundred-dollar tip on the counter.

'I'll be telling all my friends about you. The resort's great, but *Hebe* is the best part of it for me.'

Isla slipped the money into their shared tip jar before she headed out to go and find Pippa to apologise for not turning up last night.

Her first stop was the office to see if the girls knew what Pippa's schedule was. She was in luck. Pippa was in the office talking to Sienna's Danny.

'Tess, can you tell Pippa I'd like a word when she's free?'

'Sure, love.' Tess gave her a coy look, but Isla pretended not to notice.

For fecks' sake, is nothing private on this island? Or am I imagining that everyone knows how I spent the night?

Isla went into the kitchen and made herself a cup of tea to take to the veranda while she waited for Pippa. Focusing on her work for the past hour had calmed her, but she yawned as she pulled out a chair. She hadn't had much sleep last night in Ronan's bed. Her face heated as she remembered what an incredible night they had spent together. Never in her life had she felt so close to another human being.

But it had all been a lie.

She closed her eyes trying to deal with the knowledge that Ronan had used her, but hurt pierced her heart. He'd be gone from the island as soon as he finished his contract, and she would just have to deal with him being here until then. She would stay away from him and ignore him.

I am not running again, she vowed to herself. *Unless I have to.*

As Isla lifted the teacup, a cross voice come from the office. 'Yes, I need to know now. It is *extremely* important.'

Her heart thudded and her whole body tensed. She dropped her cup into the saucer with a clatter as the flight instinct took over, and coffee splashed down the front of her white uniform.

No way. She was just on edge.

'How exactly can I help you?' Tess's voice was quiet and patient, totally at odds with the crazy feelings that were taking over Isla.

It couldn't be. Her hands were like ice, and she couldn't stop shaking as disbelief flooded through her. It was just a woman with an Irish accent.

'I'd like to know if you have a guest on the island by the name of Ronan Doyle, please.'

That voice took Isla back many years. Whining at the kitchen table when Isla was too slow eating her breakfast, and they were running late for the school bus. Teasing her when she didn't get invited to Mary Malone's birthday party because she wasn't in the cool group at school. And then later, only hearing her sister's voice when she talked to their parents, because Marlene was a cool university student who didn't waste her breath on a teenage sister.

A multitude of feelings surfaced in Isla as she sat there glued to the chair. She gripped the table as Tess answered. 'I'm sorry, Mrs Kendall, but Mr Doyle is no longer a guest here. But I can get a message to him if you would like to leave one.'

Mrs Kendall? *Good, it wasn't her.* Her mind was doing her head in since Ronan had shown his true colours.

'Thank you. Please tell him that Marlene Kendall is on the island and needs to speak to him as a matter of urgency.'

Isla gagged. She managed to stand and walk along the veranda to the back of the house before running down the steps.

God, the last person she wanted to see was her sister. Despite the fast-building heat of the morning her hands stayed cold and her legs barely supported her as she hurried across the lawn, no destination in mind. She just needed to get away, out of sight somewhere.

'Isla!' Pippa's voice followed her, and Isla closed her eyes.

'Isla, wait up!'

Isla stopped in the middle of the lawn at the back of the house and waited for Pippa to reach her.

'Sorry, Isla, I wanted to catch you before you went back to work. I'm sorry I wasn't available last night. We had some issues with the computer system and Gabe needed me in the office.'

Isla put her hand on her chest. 'Oh, that makes me feel better. To be honest, I forgot. We— I—was busy and didn't give it a thought. It doesn't matter, I have to go now.'

'That worked out well then. You haven't got time to come back to the office now?'

'No. I mean, yes.' Isla shook her head. 'But not the office. Can we just talk here?' She spoke quickly and her words ran together. Distracted by Pippa, she glanced over her shoulder to make sure no one else was coming. Pippa gently took her arm and steered her towards the low building in front of them.

Isla hadn't been in there before and looked around nervously. 'Do the guests come in here?'

'No, it's Odessa's studio.' Pippa frowned. 'Isla, what's wrong? You're as tense as anything.'

Isla was embarrassed when tears filled her eyes. She wasn't used to anyone worrying about her, or how she was feeling. She sniffed and pulled a tissue out of her uniform pocket. 'I'm sorry. I just didn't want that woman to see me. I don't want her to know that I work here.'

'Is there a problem? I noticed her Irish accent. Do you know her?'

'Unfortunately, I do.' Isla nodded and dabbed at her eyes. 'Marlene's my sister but I haven't seen her since I left Ireland almost ten years ago. And I don't want to.'

'Do you think she knows you're here? Or could it be a coincidence?'

'Not if she was looking for Ronan, like she said.' Her voice was bitter. 'I'm sorry, Pippa. You don't want to get involved in my problems. I'll be fine. I'll keep a very low profile while she's on the island.'

'Is that what you wanted to see me about?'

'Oh, no. Of course not. I wouldn't involve you. Just forget about it.'

They walked through the workshop to a small sitting room at the back, and Pippa gestured to the low sofa under the window. 'Sit down, Isla.' She smiled and her voice was quiet. 'This sofa was the original from my great aunt's house back in the 1930s or 40s. I'm not sure exactly how old it is, but it's seen lots of tears and heard many secrets.' She reached out and Isla looked down when Pippa took her hand. 'You're really pale, love. Please tell me how I can help. That's what we do here. We all look out for each other, and we take care of each other when there's a problem. And you obviously have something difficult that you're dealing with. I'd like to be able to help.'

'Please don't worry about my ... my family stuff.' Isla sniffed and wiped her nose. 'I just wanted to know if I've passed my probationary month. I was getting a bit worried.'

'Oh, no need to. My brain seems to have gone to mush the last couple of weeks. That totally slipped my mind. Of course, you're staying. We love having you here and the feedback from the *Hebe* clients has been awesome. I'm so sorry. With the wedding and then sharing our baby news, I've been preoccupied.'

'Thank you.'

'You will stay, won't you? We'd like you to.'

'I'd like to as well.' Isla looked around. 'I'll be honest. It does depend on a few things though.' She didn't know what that might be, but if things got too hard, she would leave the island if she had to. But she didn't want to.

'Well, if there's anything I can do, just let me know. Do you know why your sister was looking for Ronan? Does she know him?'

'Apparently she does, but I don't know how. Time will tell.'

'I've been really pleased to see you and Ronan spending time together.'

'No more,' Isla said fiercely and jumped to her feet. 'I'm sorry. I have to go. I have a client due in soon.'

'Okay. Now if you want to talk some more, you know where to find me.' Pippa's eyes were full of concern. 'I mean that. You come and find me. At the house. Any time of the day or night.'

Chapter Thirty-Two
Ronan

Sienna's face held no expression as she stood by *Hebe's* counter. She'd been with a client but had come out to see who had opened the sliding door. Ronan stood in the doorway and looked around the foyer of the day spa.

'Good morning, Ronan. Do you wish to make another appointment?'

He shook his head. 'No, thank you. Not yet. I'm looking for Isla. Is she here?'

'No, she's gone over to the main office.'

'Thanks, I'll go and catch her on the way back.'

As he turned to go Sienna caught his arm. 'Just so you know, Isla looked very upset when she arrived this morning.'

'I thought she might have been, that's why I need to talk to her. As soon as I can.'

Before she can disappear again, he thought. But this time it had nothing to do with the assignment he'd been given; it was because Ronan couldn't bear the thought of losing Isla. And knowing that she thought badly of him.

Jesus, what had she thought when she'd scrolled though his camera? There were dozens and dozens of photos of her. Most taken with his telephoto lens. In about three different locations that she would recognise.

Did Isla have any idea that her sister was searching for her? When Isla had been honest with him about her difficult past, he should have opened up then and told her the truth.

Sienna's eyes were full of sympathy as she reached out and lightly touched his arm. 'Go and find her. Whatever the problem is, be truthful. Don't let there be any room for misunderstanding.' She looked down at her left hand and smiled, and Ronan noticed the flash of diamonds, but he didn't comment.

'I will, thank you. And I'll sort it out.'

'She won't be long. She has an appointment shortly.'

Ronan nodded and headed out the door. There was no sign of anyone coming along the path, so he sat on one of the garden bench seats that had been built around the tree trunks. From where he sat in the sun-dappled glade, he could see the front steps of *Hebe* as well as back along the path to the house where the office was located. Only a few minutes passed before the sound of someone walking along the track reached him. He stood and waited, and when the sunlight shone on the white uniform, he knew it was Isla.

Her head was down as she approached, and the last thing he wanted to do was spook her. He rose and stood still and quiet as she got closer.

When she had almost reached him, Ronan stepped forward. 'Isla, I need to talk to you.'

She lifted her chin and scowled at him. Regret pummelled his chest as her cold stare suggested he had just crawled out from under a rock.

'Cop onto yourself, you scut. See these?' Isla placed both hands over her ears. 'I don't want to hear a word from your lying mouth. You feckin' jackeen.'

'I'm sorry, I've never heard that term before.' He tried to keep his voice quiet.

'You haven't? Well, let me enlighten you. It means an obnoxious piece of shite.' She pushed past him, and her cold stare almost broke his heart. The warm and loving woman who had laughed with him through the most glorious night of his life had morphed into someone who hated him.

And he couldn't blame her, but he needed to explain.

'Now let me through. *I* have to go to work. But I guess you're on holidays now. Your job here is done, hey boyo?'

'Isla, please listen to me. Once I was sure who you were, and realised you didn't want to be found, I emailed my client and told them it wasn't you, and I quit. I—'

'Ronan, didn't you hear what I said? I don't want to talk to you and I don't want to hear your lies.'

'I'm not lying. I need to explain. Isla, I—'

'You're not lying? Bollocks! Poor little Irishman who didn't take enough water on his walk so I felt sorry for you. The loving family boyo who made up a whole family in Dingle just to get my interest. And then, and then you had the gall to entice me into your bloody bed. You say you're not lying, then why the feck is my sister in reception asking for you? I can't imagine anyone except for my family who would have put you up to this.'

'Your sister?' Ronan's hope of making her listen disintegrated with those two words.

'Yes, my sister.' Isla turned on her heel and ran towards the day spa hut. 'Just feck off out of my life!'

Chapter Thirty-Three

Isla drew in a deep shuddering breath as she pushed open the front door of the day spa. Sienna's treatment room was in use, and she let out her breath with a sigh of relief. She didn't want to talk to anyone. She couldn't talk to anyone without cracking. Not until she came to grips with her feelings. Could this day get any worse?

It had been bloody hard not to give in and listen to Ronan, and hear his feeble excuses, but she knew to survive she had to be strong. As much as she wanted to give in and let him hold her, she couldn't.

She couldn't *trust* him. Like everyone else in her life, Ronan had let her down, and in the worst way possible. He had lied to her.

Even though Niall had let her down, he had always been truthful, and as for Da? Well, Isla had always known where she stood with him.

The lowest of the low. The daughter who was a disappointment and never good enough. She blinked away tears. Maybe she shouldn't have given in and let her parents organise the termination of her pregnancy. Maybe she should have told the counsellor, no, I want to have a child! Someone who would love her, and someone who she could care about.

Maybe if she had, and had sought out Niall back then, her life would have been very different.

Maybe he would have married her, and she would be the wife who lived with him in that beautiful house in Dublin and she would have had more of his children. They would have lived in the house with the happy family she had seen when she had found him on Facebook five years ago.

Isla couldn't even remember where she had been when she had seen it. The image had stayed in her mind and had sent her into a downward spiral for months.

But since she had met Sienna on Esculanta Island, she had been happy and was looking forward to staying and working on Pentecost Island. She *loved* it here, and she wasn't going anywhere. She felt valued for the first time in her life.

The sooner Ronan Doyle removed himself from the island and her life, and left her in peace the better, she told herself.

But a small part of her heart disagreed.

'Isla?'

Isla lifted her head quickly. Sienna had come out of her room, and Isla hadn't even heard the door open.

'Sorry. I was miles away.'

'Are you all right?' Sienna's voice was soft.

Isla nodded. 'I'm okay. I have to get organised now. I have a client in a few minutes.'

'Okay, as long as you're fine.'

'I am. But I tell you what, I could sure do with a sunset drink on the beach tonight.'

Sienna reached up and pushed her hair back from her forehead.

Isla widened her eyes. 'My God, Sienna! Is that an engagement ring on your hand? It is! Why didn't you tell me?'

Sienna's cheeks flushed and she nodded. 'I thought you were unhappy, and I didn't want to make you feel worse.'

Isla stepped over and hugged her friend. 'Don't be silly. I'm so happy for you. I'm fine. My little hiccup is over. Done and dusted. Time to move on. But tell me, when did this happen?' She picked up Sienna's left hand and looked at the ring. 'It's beautiful.'

'The other night.' Sienna's smile was wide, and a tiny burst of jealousy bloomed in Isla's heart, but she pushed it down. 'When I was hoping that's what Danny had planned. And he did.'

'All the more reason for a celebration tonight!' Isla kept her voice bright and upbeat.

'Let's talk to the others this afternoon, and see if they have plans,' Sienna said. 'There's a lot happening on the island at the moment.'

'Sure, let's do that.'

The door of the treatment room opened and Sienna's client stepped out.

'Back to work,' Isla said quietly.

The front door slid open and she looked up. Her heart thudded and her legs shook as she looked into the face of the sister she hadn't seen for over ten years.

Unable to speak, Isla nodded briefly and opened the door of her room. Sienna frowned and crossed to the reception counter, and as Isla closed the door and leaned her back against it, she closed her eyes listening to Sienna welcoming the "client".

'Please take a seat, Isla is just preparing the room, and will be with you shortly.'

Panic gripped her, and Isla looked to the small window opposite the massage table wondering if she could climb out and simply disappear into the forest.

This was all Ronan's fault.

A light tap on the door had her jumping forward.

'Isla? That is your client waiting.'

'Yes, thank you. Please tell her I will only be a moment.' Isla crossed to the sink and ran a flannel under the hot water. She placed it over her eyes for a few seconds and then when it cooled, she pressed the flannel against her hot cheeks.

Crossing to the mirror beside the table, she pulled her hair back and tightened the clip securing her curls, and then smoothed her uniform with shaking hands.

Taking a deep breath, she opened the door and stepped out.

'Hello Marlene, I won't lie and say it's been too long, but it has been a long time. Come in. and we'll get this over and done with.'

Her older sister followed her into the room.

Chapter Thirty-Four
Pippa

Sometimes, the days went so quickly, I didn't know how we got everything done on the island. Guests came and went every day, and there was always something new to focus on. This week Eliza and I had been working closely with Ronan to put the finishing touches on our new promotion package. Eliza had had the crazy idea of entering us in the state tourism awards.

'It's too soon,' I had protested. 'We'll be a laughingstock of the industry.'

But I couldn't budge her, and Ronan had agreed it was a good idea too. As I walked back to the office after Isla had left me, I consciously focused on my breathing. A visit to the bathroom was an essential stop first; I had been drinking lots of water as the late summer sun—and my pregnancy—sapped my energy.

Seeing Isla upset had worried me, and I'd make sure that I found her later when she had finished her appointments for the day. Not only had her sister turned up here, but it seemed as though her close friendship with Ronan—or more, according to the island grapevine—had hit a rocky patch.

I was happy, and I wanted everyone on the island to be happy. Eliza and I had a meeting with him now to discuss the progress of his photographic work for the current promotion, and I'd dig gently and see what I could do to help. After I came out of the newly renovated bathroom—oh, how I wished Aunty Vi could have seen it—he and Eliza were waiting in the small office that Renzo had added to the back of the veranda. Even though the layout of the rooms and the décor had changed—I still caught myself walking towards doorways that were no longer there—the house had retained its beautiful character. Sometimes I would walk up the steps and half expect Aunty Vi to be waiting there for me.

'Hi Pip. We were just getting a coffee. Would you like one?' Eliza stood behind Ronan who was sitting on the small sofa in the office. She gestured down to him and frowned.

'No, thanks,' I said catching her eye and giving a small nod. 'I'm drinking herbal tea now. Smells and tastes foul, but it's better for the baby. If there's a herbal tea bag in the kitchen, I'll have one of those please.'

'I'll get it for you. White tea with two for you, Ronan?'

'Yes, please.' His voice was dull, and his hands were clenched between his knees as he looked down.

I sat in the low chair on the other side of the coffee table and leaned back. 'So, Ronan, how are the photos going? Every time I've been somewhere on the island, I've seen you there with your camera. And your camera assistant.' I looked sideways at him.

'Yeah, it's going well.' He sat up straight and finally looked over at me. The poor guy looked totally miserable, and I couldn't let it go.

'You don't look very happy. Is there anything I can do?'

He shook his head and colour crept up his neck. 'Thanks, but no. I've done enough as it is. I'm going to get this contract finished quickly and I'll hand the photographs over to you. I think it would be best if I leave the island as soon as I can.'

'Is it because of Isla?' I hurried on to explain myself. 'Look, I'm not worried about your photos or her work. I'm worried about her. And you too, Ronan. For the past month you pair have seemed inseparable, and you looked so happy together.'

'We were, but I stuffed it up. Big time.'

I smiled at him. 'Men are good at doing that. Just give her a few days, and then make a peace offering.'

He shook his head again. 'I'll be gone by then. And it's not that easy. She'll never forgive me for what I did, and that's what I deserve. I should have been honest with her from the get-go.'

'Rubbish, don't be a wimp. The last thing you need to do is take off. Would it help to talk about it? Maybe I can help you sort it out?'

Eliza was standing in the doorway with a tray holding our drinks. 'Sorry to eavesdrop, but I agree with Pippa. I think we can help. That's if you want us to.'

For the first time Ronan's expression brightened. 'Do you think you could talk to her?'

'How about you tell us your story and we'll see what we can do to help,' I said.

Chapter Thirty-Five
Isla

'You didn't know?' Isla sat across from her sister where she sat with clients before she left them to prepare for their treatment. 'You really and truly didn't know?' Her hand shook as she picked up the glass of water.

'Isla, I had no idea. All I was ever told was that Da took you over to London because you'd decided to go to university there.'

'Bloody liar.' Isla snorted. 'He kept up the façade that I would go to university, did he?'

'That's what he told me, and then after that when I would ask, he would say you had made your choice and you didn't want anything more to do with the family. I should have tried harder to contact you. I'm so sorry. What you've told me is just dreadful. But he was a hard man, always.'

Isla's throat closed. 'He left me in a London street, outside the abortion clinic with five hundred pounds clutched in my hand. I spent weeks in a mental health facility.' Isla put her hand over her eyes as she spoke. 'Why can't he just leave me to get on with my life? Why is he chasing me now? I'm a strong woman these days, but this week has been absolute shite.' The feel of her sister's hand on her other arm had her lifting her hand away from her face.

'Isla, you don't know—' Marlene's fingers gripped her wrist. 'Da and Mam are both gone.'

'Gone? Gone where?' she asked.

'They've both passed on.'

Isla opened her mouth in shock. 'You mean they died?'

'Yes. That's why I've been looking for you. And that's why I hired Ronan Doyle to find you. He had a good reputation, and when he sent me your photo, and I knew he'd found you here on this island, I was really pleased. And then he emailed and said it wasn't you, that he was mistaken, and he was ending our contract. And I had no idea what was going on, because I knew it was you from the photo.'

'He did that?' Isla couldn't help the little spurt of joy.

'Yes, and I have no idea why. Because I knew it was you. So, I decided to travel here and see for myself.'

'I don't understand why you needed to.'

Marlene looked away. 'It started off as a legal matter, but Isla, I need to tell you that I'm really pleased to have found you, and to have learned the truth. I hope you can forgive me for abandoning you for all of those years.'

Isla waved her hand. 'We were never close, Marlene, so why should you have worried?'

'Because I knew what Da could be like and how Mam followed him blindly, no matter what he did. You were treated horrendously, and I hope I can make it up to you.'

'It's not your responsibility.'

'It is. And I have to tell you why I needed to find you. It might upset you, but I'd rather you knew the truth.'

Isla sighed but she sat up straighter. 'Upset me? I don't think anything could make the day worse. Hit me with it.'

'Two years ago, Da had a stroke while he was driving back from the office one night and the car was a wreck. He only lived for a couple of days, but Mam was in the car with him, and although she was badly hurt, she recovered. But never fully. To be honest, I think she was so used to being bossed around by him, and doing as he wanted, without him she was lost.'

Isla stared at her sister.

'Da had cut you out of his will, but not long before she died, Mam redid her will, and she told me that she had made sure that you were to get half of the estate. She was really sad, and said the way you had been treated wasn't fair. I thought she meant in the will. I didn't know any of that other stuff.'

'I don't want it.'

'It's been bequeathed to you.

'I don't want it. I don't want any memory of those days. I'm happy enough here and I have enough money for what I need. I've supported myself around the world for the past ten years, and I can keep doing that.'

But do I want to keep doing it? Isla wondered.

Her sister shook her head. 'You have to. The estate can't be finalised until you do. Take it and do whatever you want with it.'

'Because until I do you can't get your share? Is that why you travelled halfway across the world to find me? Why you hired an Irishman to find me?'

Her sister had the grace to look embarrassed. 'That's part of it. But Isla, honestly, I am so pleased to have found you. I'd like . . . I'd like for us to stay in touch.'

Isla lifted her chin. 'Why?'

Marlene reached out again. 'I'd like my two girls to meet their Aunty Aisling. I'd like you to be a part of our family. I know it might be hard to forgive, but I'd like to make it up to you.' As she held Isla's hand, a smile crept over her face. 'I think you would get on very well with Claire, my youngest. She is very much like you were when you were a teenager.' Marlene chuckled. 'She's doing my head in.'

'Poor kid,' Isla said.

'No. I used to envy you. You were so strong and you knew what you wanted. You wouldn't take any of Da's bullying. I didn't want to do law, but I did as I was told.' She held Isla's gaze. 'I haven't practised since I had the girls. Please come home and meet them. There's nothing there to hurt you anymore. If you don't I'll bring them Down Under later in the year.'

'I'll think about it. I have some things to do here first. How long are you on the island for?' Isla looked up at the clock. 'I have another client due in, and I'm busy all afternoon.' She took a breath. 'Perhaps we could have dinner together.'

Marlene smiled at her. 'I'd like that very much.'

Chapter Thirty-Six
Ronan

Ronan felt more hopeful as he left the office after talking to Pippa and Eliza. He walked along the path to his hut, wondering how long it would be before Isla would listen to him. It was so hot he could see the waves of heat shimmering above the sand on the beach. He pulled his handkerchief from his shorts pocket and mopped at his brow. How did anyone live in this heat?

Pippa and Eliza had reassured him. Both women had listened sympathetically as he'd told them the story of being hired to find Isla.

'Yes, you stuffed up,' Pippa said.

Eliza nodded. 'And at least you recognise that yourself. It takes a big man to admit that he made a mistake.'

'But Isla won't listen to me. She won't believe me that I told her sister that the woman I found wasn't her.'

Pippa had put one finger to her lips. 'You have strong feelings for her? For Isla, I mean.'

'Of course I do. If I didn't care about her, I would have left as soon as I told her sister she was here.'

Pippa nodded. 'Yes, the sister. Another complication to be overcome. Isla told me she was here, and I could see she was worried. Okay, if she won't talk to you, leave it with us. I don't want to see anyone unhappy on our island.'

Eliza had reached over and squeezed his hand reassuringly. 'Trust us, Ronan. Okay? They don't call Pentecost Island the "Island of Love" for nothing.'

Perspiration trickled down his neck as he approached his hut. He would get his camera and take some more shots of the rainforest; it might be cooler in there. Then again, he could stay in the air-conditioned bar, and try to figure out how to convince Isla that he *had* told the truth. It was good of Pippa and Eliza to offer to help, but it was up to him.

As Ronan wrestled with a decision, he turned onto the path towards the bar.

'About feckin' time you came back, boyo.'

His head flew up and he stopped as he stared into the dim forest. Isla was sitting in the shade on the seat underneath the spreading tree before the pool area.

'Hello,' he said cautiously. 'I'm pleased to see you. I think.'

'Make up your mind.'

He nodded. 'I am. Very pleased. Were you taking a rest in the heat, or could I dare hope you were waiting for me?'

'I was waiting for you.'

'I thought you had appointments all day?'

'Sienna took my next one for me. She had a cancellation. Come and sit by me. I need to talk to you.'

Ronan sat beside her and, as he looked at Isla, he realised she was as nervous as he was.

'I owe you an apology,' she said. 'I should have listened to you, but I was upset. I'm sorry for yelling at you and calling you all those names.'

'No. It's me who must apologise. I should have told you the truth. I should have told you that I had emailed your sister. I really did, Isla.'

'I know. She told me.'

'Thank the heavens for that.'

'I should have trusted you, but I'm not very good at trusting.'

'Maybe it's time you had someone in your life who could teach you how to trust.'

'Do you think so?' She moved closer to him. 'Maybe it is.'

Ronan lifted his arm and put it around Isla's shoulder. 'There's just one thing you need to know before you make up your mind.'

'What's that?' Isla turned her face up to his and put one hand on his cheek.

He lowered his head so that his lips hovered over hers. 'I really do come from Dingle, and if you decide to accept me as a part of your life, you'll have to put up with my family. A large family.'

'You'll have to teach me how to be a part of a family.'

Ronan closed his eyes as happiness and relief surged through him.

'And Ronan? I've found *my* family today,' she said.

He smiled against her lips as Isla's arms went around his neck and pulled him close. There would be plenty of time later for her to find out that her island family was watching out for her too.

'*Macushla,*' he said softly before his lips claimed hers.

Epilogue
Pippa – Five months later

Even though my childhood in Brisbane, before I had moved up to live with Aunty Vi, had been tragic and difficult, I had some special memories that I cherished. My friendship with Tam and Nell since that swimming carnival when I had won a ribbon in Grade 4, and the memories of my special times with my mum. For the twelve short years of my life I had a mother, I adored her. We spent a lot of time home alone because Dad worked down on the oil rigs in Bass Strait; he was one of the first fly-in-fly-out workers before it became commonplace.

One lovely Sunday afternoon in the winter before she . . . died, Mum took me to where the old Cloudland ballroom had been in Bowen Hills. It had been demolished without a permit one night before I was born, but Mum had shared with me how she had met my father there. We had danced along the footpath and she had sung me a whole set of seventies songs, and the memory of that day was as clear as if it had been yesterday, twenty years later.

A new Cloudland had been created not far from the original site, and the annual state tourism awards were being held at the venue. So I guess being here tonight for the awards ceremony had brought me full circle.

Now that I had Rafe and I was going to be a mother, I could understand a little more of what had made my mum the way she was.

The week before Dad came home every second month, there was always a mad flurry in the house. The rooms all smelled like furniture polish and baby violets filled tiny little vases on every space. The kitchen benches were covered with fresh-baked bikkies and cakes cooling on wire racks.

I loved that week because the rest of the time, we lived in chaos and made do with bought biscuits and takeaway food.

I guess I did get more from Mum than the ginger hair. I vowed that I would show our child how much I loved him . . . or her.

'Are you okay, Pip?' Rafe held my hand tightly as we walked behind Nat and Nell. 'You're very quiet. No pains or anything.'

My pregnancy was too advanced for flying down to Brisbane—there was only a week before our baby was due to arrive—so Rafe and I had taken two days to drive down. I wasn't going to miss this ceremony for anything. Ma Carmichael's Resort had been nominated in three categories.

I squeezed his hand back. 'Just thinking about growing up in Brisbane.' I grinned as I looked ahead at Tam and Gabe, who were pushing a double stroller holding their three-month-old twins, Harriet and Thomas, and at Nell and Nat, who were holding their six-week-old daughter, Lee-Anne, who had the loudest cry I had ever heard. 'And thinking how grateful I am to our friends who've all contributed to bringing our resort this far. I just wish they could have all come tonight.'

'Someone has to run Ma Carmichael's.' he said.

'True,' I said.

'We'll take lots of photos, and I think Ronan is going to video the parts we're nominated for,' Eliza said as she and Phillipe caught up to us.

We caught up to the rest of our group and Dylan pointed to the large circular table we were all sitting at. I was pleased that Odessa had been able to come as they were flying to England in the morning to show off her engagement ring to Jenny and Bryant, her parents.

I had asked for a table near the exit, so Tam and Nell could make an easy exit if the babies needed attention. It was also close to the ladies' room for me; I'd seemed to live in the loo the past week.

'Are you excited, Pippa?' Isla asked as she stood next to Ronan at the table.

'I am,' I said with a smile for them both. 'Our nominations are because of the wonderful work your man did, Isla.'

'Don't sell yourself short, Pippa. The nominations are because of your wonderful resort you created. I just took the photos of what you created.' Ronan held Isla close to him. They had moved in together to one of the double rooms in the staff lodge and they both seemed very happy. Ronan had agreed to work with us part time on promotion, and he'd picked up some more photographic work with the local tourism body at Airlie Beach.

Before I could reply to Ronan, Tamsin turned to me with a grin. 'Nice evening dress, girlfriend. If you didn't know you were pregnant . . .'

'Ha ha. If they didn't know, anyone could guess by taking one look at my huge belly.' I put my hand on the olive-green silk that was straining across my stomach. The dress had fitted last week, when I had picked it up, but I had expanded in those five days.

'You look gorgeous, Pip.' Nell reached across and hugged me. 'My God, is that baby still kicking?'

We all sat down at the table as the MC on the stage asked everyone to take their seats, and we were soon eating our meal and watching a slideshow of all the nominated resorts, restaurants and tourist attractions.

'Look, there we are!' I clapped my hands together as a fabulous drone shot of Pentecost Island filled the screen. The oohs and ahs from the audience sent a thrill through me.

Rafe leaned over and kissed my cheek. 'You've done very well, sweetheart.'

'We've all done very well.' I drew in my breath as a sudden ache gripped my lower back, but I didn't say anything. It went away slowly and didn't come back.

After dessert was served, the presentation of the awards began, and Tamsin and Nell's little cherubs stayed fast asleep. Motherhood was going to be a breeze, I thought.

I was chuffed when *Violet's,* our restaurant, received the highly commended award in Excellence in Customer Experience - Restaurants

I was astounded when *Hebe*, our day spa was runner up in the Excellence in Customer Experience Boutique Service category. Eliza accepted the silver award for us.

As I leaned closer to Rafe, another ache held me in its vice briefly, and I paused before I spoke to him. He was looking at the small, carved award that Eliza had passed around the table and didn't notice me hesitate.

'I am so proud,' I finally managed to get out. 'I can't believe we've won two awards and we're just coming up to our second anniversary.'

'It's not over yet,' my husband said.

The lights dimmed and there was a drum roll as the Minister for Tourism held up the envelope for the highest award for the night.

'I have much pleasure in announcing the winner for Excellence in Customer Experience, Hotel and Resort Accommodation.' Opening the envelope, he read it and leaned towards the microphone. 'And the winner is Ma Carmichael's Resort on Pentecost Island in our beautiful Whitsunday region.'

I don't recall how I got to the stage, but when I got there, I was flanked by my best friends, Tamsin, Nell and Eliza. We were all in shock, and as we stood there, the spotlight hit our table and tears rolled down my cheeks when I saw the look on Rafe's face. He stood proudly beside Nat and Gabe—who were each holding a baby, and on his other side was Odessa, holding Tam and Gabe's other twin.

The Minister shook my hand, and I was asked to say a few words.

I stood in front of the microphone ignoring the ache building in my lower back.

'Two years ago, three friends came to Pentecost Island,'—I smiled through my tears—'now also known as the "Island of Love". Together we worked hard, and our friendship circle grew as more good people joined us. It is the love and commitment of each one of those people I am proud to call my friends that has created the wonderful resort that we now have. Thank you.' I held the gold trophy aloft and leaned closer to the microphone as I clutched my stomach. 'I just have one more thing to say. Rafe, I think we need to find a hospital.'

Our perfect little daughter, Violet Adele Rendell arrived safely just over an hour later.

I watched Rafe as he stared down at her face, his expression full of awe. 'I told you we were going to have a little girl and she's beautiful, just like her mother.' He leaned down and brushed his lips over mine, and then on our daughter's forehead. 'And look, her hair is the same apricot colour as yours.'

'And look at her eyes,' I whispered. 'She has her father's eyes.'

##

Two weeks later, on a warm afternoon in spring, Tasmin, Nell, Eliza and I stood on the beach as the sun hovered over the mountains in the west. The sky faded from that deep indigo blue into an array of pinks shot with gold, and the only sound was the small waves breaking on the shingly sand.

I lifted my glass of soda water. 'To friendship, girls. To the unbreakable bond that has seen us stay together through the ups and downs of our lives. And the friendships and love that has created our wonderful resort. All for one and one for all.'

'All for one, and one for all,' they replied.

As the sun slipped slowly towards the sea, we sat there in silence, each lost in our own thoughts of the past two years. All that we had achieved, the love that we had found—our partners, our children, and together, the resort we had created thanks to my dear Aunty Vi—Ma Carmichael's Resort.

I looked up at the fading sky and the first star of the evening twinkled at me. I smiled and raised my glass to Aunty Vi.

THE END

I hope you've enjoyed meeting the Pentecost Island girls.

Watch out for the new Outback series that will follow.

Come on over and join my newsletter on my website to keep up to date with my releases.

https://www.annieseaton.net/

Other Books

Whitsunday Dawn

Undara

Osprey Reef (2021)

East of Alice (2022)

Porter Sisters Series

Kakadu Sunset

Daintree

Diamond Sky

Hidden Valley

Larapinta (2022)

Pentecost Island Series

Pippa

Eliza

Nell

Tamsin

Evie

Cherry

Odessa

Sienna

Tess

Isla

Sunshine Coast Series

Waiting for Ana

The Trouble with Jack

Healing His Heart

Bondi Beach Love Series

Beach House

Beach Music

Beach Walk

Beach Dreams

The House on the Hill

Second Chance Bay Series

Her Outback Playboy

Her Outback Protector

Her Outback Haven

Her Outback Paradise

Love Across Time Series

Come Back to Me

Follow Me

Finding Home

The Threads that Bind

Others

The Trouble with Paradise

Deadly Secrets

Adventures in Time

Silver Valley Witch

The Emerald Necklace

Worth the Wait

Ten Days in Paradise

All books are also available in print from:

https://www.annieseaton.net/store.html

Acknowledgements

Thank you to my editor, Susanne Bellamy, and my proof-readers, Roby Aiken and Kristen Woolgar.

About the Author

Finalist for the NZ KORU award 2018 and 2020.

Winner ...Best Established Author of the Year 2017 AUSROM

Long listed for the Sisters in Crime Davitt Awards 2016, 2017, 2018, 2019

Finalist in Book of the Year, Long Romance, RWA Ruby awards 2016

Winner ...Best Established Author of the Year 2015 AUSROM

Winner ...Author of the Year 2014 AUSROM

Best Established Author, Ausrom Readers' Choice 2017

Book of the Year (Whitsunday Dawn) Ausrom Readers' Choice Awards 2018

Annie lives in Australia, on the beautiful north coast of New South Wales. She sits in her writing chair and looks out over the tranquil Pacific Ocean. She has fulfilled her lifelong dream of becoming an author and is producing books at a prolific rate.

She writes contemporary romance and loves telling the stories that always have a happily Ever after. She lives with her very own hero of many years and they share their home with Toby, the naughtiest dog in the universe, and Barney, the rag doll puss, who hides when the grandchildren come to visit.

Stay up to date with her latest releases at her website: http://www.annieseaton.net

www.ingramcontent.com/pod-product-compliance
Lightning Source LLC
Chambersburg PA
CBHW050144120726
47903CB00002B/482